"Will you marry me?"

Pulling free, Cassandra turned and walked briskly back along the path they'd just taken.

"Cassie, wait a minute." Jared grasped her arm and halted her. "At least discuss it," he said.

"What's to discuss? I won't be a baby-sitter for the rest of my life. All you want is a mother for the girls. A woman doesn't want to be married unless she's loved and cherished."

"Don't say no tonight, Cassie. Think about it."

"I don't need to think about it, I—" Before Cassandra could finish her sentence, Jared covered her mouth with his. It was as if she had been waiting especially for his touch. He forgot the burden of becoming a father, forgot about the demands of the office. The only reality was the petite woman in his arms and the fire her kisses fed.

At last he ___ bemused ___ and bribe ___ her for the mother ___ he'd make sure he got her.

Welcome to **DADDY BOOM!**

Just look who's holding the baby now! Following on from our highly popular BABY BOOM series, Harlequin Romance® is proud to introduce a brand-new series, DADDY BOOM, full of babies, bachelors and happy-ever-afters. Meet irresistible heroes who are about to discover that there's a first time for everything—even fatherhood!

Second in our series is *Daddy and Daughters* by Barbara McMahon. We'll be bringing you one deliciously cute DADDY BOOM title every other month.

Look out in June for *Falling for Jack*, by Trisha David.

DADDY BOOM

Who says bachelors and babies don't mix?

Daddy and Daughters
Barbara McMahon

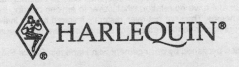

HARLEQUIN®

TORONTO • NEW YORK • LONDON
AMSTERDAM • PARIS • SYDNEY • HAMBURG
STOCKHOLM • ATHENS • TOKYO • MILAN • MADRID
PRAGUE • WARSAW • BUDAPEST • AUCKLAND

ISBN 0-373-03547-0

DADDY AND DAUGHTERS

First North American Publication 1999.

Copyright © 1999 by Barbara McMahon.

This edition published by arrangement with Harlequin Books S.A.

® and TM are trademarks of the publisher. Trademarks indicated with ® are registered in the United States Patent and Trademark Office, the Canadian Trade Marks Office and in other countries.

Printed in U.S.A.

CHAPTER ONE

JARED HUNTER took a deep breath as the elevator doors slid open. Stepping into the large open office filled with workstations and desks, he looked straight ahead, toward his private office in the far corner. For a moment he wished he had postponed this. His briefcase gripped in one hand, he began the long walk, ignoring the heads that turned his way.

"Sorry about Mrs. Hunter," Jeb called from his station.

Julie Myers stood as he passed her desk, her features serious and sad. "I'm so sorry, Jared," she said softly.

He nodded grimly and kept walking. Still dazed by the turn of events, he longed for the sanctity of his office. It was hard to believe MaryEllen was dead. He didn't realize people died from pneumonia these days. With all the fancy medicines in the world, they couldn't have stopped the devastation of such an old disease?

"Jared, are you all right?" Helen Walter, his secretary, rose from her desk outside his door and moved toward him. Her eyes brimmed with sympathy.

Jared nodded. "It was a bitch of a trip, but at least I'm home now. How are things here?" He clenched his jaw, feeling the strain. It wouldn't get easier.

"Morale is down. But with the rapid expansion over the last three years, only the old-timers actually knew MaryEllen. Still, many of the employees have talked to her on the phone, and everyone knew she was the other partner."

5

Noticing she'd avoided the obvious, that MaryEllen had also been his wife, Jared wearily pushed open the door and entered his office. Mail was stacked in neat piles on the right side of his desk. A small mound of folders sat on the far left side. Pink phone messages were centered with a long cream-colored envelope across them.

He rounded the desk and dropped his briefcase on the credenza behind his chair. The view of San Francisco Bay sparkling in the afternoon sunshine went unnoticed as he surveyed the work waiting. God, he was tired!

"You just get in?" Helen asked, hovering in the doorway.

"Flight finally landed about an hour ago. I came straight here."

"Are you really okay? I know you and MaryEllen lived three thousand miles apart these last three years, but she was your wife."

He glanced at her. "Helen, you know that was a legal technicality." He paused. "Is the gossip mill humming?"

"No more than usual. Those of us who have been here since the beginning made sure the others knew you and MaryEllen had been married purely to facilitate the start-up of Hunter Associates. I think some of the new employees didn't realize she was your wife. They never met her. She stayed in New York, you know."

He nodded. He skimmed the top message, then flicked the envelope. "What's this?" The rest of his mail had been opened and lay in one of his folders.

"I separated those messages. They've been calling every day for the last two weeks. Yesterday we received the registered letter. I tried to explain why we couldn't reach you in Bangkok. Obviously they weren't monitoring the news or they would have heard about the typhoon.''

Jared shrugged. He slipped out of his suit jacket, draped it across the back of his chair and slowly sat. ''Anyone from here attend the funeral?'' he asked.

''No. But most of the New York office went. Bob Mason sent a report. I put it in the folder with the rest of your mail. Don't blame yourself for not being there, Jared. You would have been there had it been possible. MaryEllen would have understood.''

''Why are these lawyers calling?'' Jared didn't want to discuss the reasons he had not been able to get to New York in time. He'd tried his best, but fate had decreed otherwise. It was over and done with, time to move on. His anger at fate had abated, and a philosophical calm replaced it. If anyone had understood business problems, it had been MaryEllen. She had thrived on them.

''They didn't tell me, just insisted they had to reach you. I gave them the Bangkok telephone number, so they could see for themselves why we couldn't get through. You know lawyers—not very trusting. Why they'd think we were trying to hinder communications, I don't know.''

''Thanks, Helen.''

''Let me know if you need anything.''

''Right.''

She eased the door almost shut as Jared picked up the envelope. He was dead tired. Flying through more than half a dozen time zones did that—especially after two weeks of hell. If he were a superstitious man, he'd be convinced the deal he was working on was jinxed.

The trip had started off wrong, with mechanical difficulties on the outbound airliner forcing an emergency stop on Wake Island. Then there had been the wildly bumpy flight into Bangkok, followed by a customs mixup. Bad weather plagued him from the moment he left the airport. The hotel where he had reservations had burned the night before his arrival, and he'd had to locate new lodgings before the predicted typhoon hit. He'd barely informed his office of the change in location before the high winds and torrential rains of Typhoon Initi let loose.

Severe storms did major damage in the United States, but recovery time was usually rapid. In Bangkok, it seemed interminable. He'd received word of MaryEllen's death only hours before the full force of the typhoon hit. Airplanes had been grounded, communications and electricity cut off. The streets flooded. Accidents abounded. It had been days before a semblance of normal activities could be resumed. Days before he could contact his office to notify them he would return on the first available flight.

Jared tapped the edge of the envelope on the desk, wishing he could quantify his feelings about MaryEllen's death. He shook his head, feeling vaguely impatient. They had been married for more than six years. Even though their marriage had been primarily a business arrangement she'd been a friend and one-time lover. Maybe fatigue numbed his reactions, dulled his emotions. Shock had been replaced with disbelief. She had been twenty-nine—too young to die. Especially with all she had wanted to accomplish so close to being achieved.

He hadn't seen her in over a year—and that had been when they'd met in Washington, D.C., with the congressmen from California for the discussion of Pacific

Rim trade regulations. But they talked on the phone frequently, kept in touch by e-mail and fax.

Married six years, separated by a continent for the last three of those years, it had not been much of a relationship. Except in business—MaryEllen shone in that arena. It had been her idea to expand into the European market. She'd insisted she be the one to move to New York to set up that office. From the initial discussion to her transfer things had moved like a whirlwind. Once she left San Francisco, she never looked back—never came back, even for a flying visit. And he had not missed her. Now he would, if only in business.

Jared sighed and slit open the envelope. Slowly he began to read.

Stunned, he reread the letter. Unbelievable!

"Helen!" he roared.

He read the words a third time. Was this some kind of joke? How could— "Helen!"

The door opened slightly. Jared looked into the diffident gaze of Cassandra Bowles. His mind occupied with the contents of the letter, it took him a moment to register it wasn't Helen warily watching him.

"Sorry, Jared, Helen stepped away from her desk. Can I help you?"

"Read this and tell me what it says." Jared stood and thrust out the letter.

Cassandra entered the office, carrying a thin manila folder in one hand. She had been lurking outside his door on the off chance Jared would have a few minutes in which she could discuss the GlobalNet merger. When she'd heard him call Helen, she'd looked for the secretary. When he'd called again, she felt someone should answer him.

She crossed the expanse of his office and gingerly

took the paper. Impatient, Jared ran his fingers through his hair as he studied her. Cassandra dropped her gaze to the typed letter. She had started with Hunter Associates two years ago, immediately after graduating from the MBA program at Berkeley. However, her interaction with the senior partner had been minimal. After all, he was the head of the firm, one of the two partners, and she a mere marketing analyst.

She looked at him, puzzled, unsure why he wanted her to read the letter.

"It seems the attorneys in New York are wondering when you will be coming to get your twin daughters." Was she supposed to deduce something else from the letter?

"Damn." Jared sat down, staring at Cassandra. "Twins."

Uneasily, Cassandra perched on the edge of a chair and gravely studied him. She swallowing visibly, then said, "It, um, almost sounds as if you were unaware of their existence."

"I had no idea." How could MaryEllen give birth to his daughters and not tell him?

Cassandra said nothing.

Jared rifled through the pink telephone slips. Each one from the same people—MaryEllen's attorneys in New York. Slowly he picked up one and punched in the number.

It rang endlessly.

"It's after five in New York," Cassandra said softly.

Slipping the receiver on the cradle, Jared nodded. The last thing he expected today was to discover he was a father. Or was he? Why hadn't MaryEllen told him if he were the father?

"You needed me, boss?" Helen asked from the doorway.

"Are you *sure* none of these lawyers told you why they were calling?" Jared asked, flicking an impatient finger against the stack of phone messages.

She nodded.

"Read this." He tossed the letter on the desk.

Helen glanced at Cassandra as she crossed to take the letter. Reading it, her eyes widened with surprise. "Wow, congratulations, Jared. You're a daddy."

"You think so?"

She looked puzzled. "It says so."

"You know that MaryEllen moved east almost three years ago to open the New York office. Unless she was pregnant when she left, those children aren't mine."

Helen glanced again at Cassandra. "Maybe you better wait and talk about this later. After you call the attorneys."

"I tried them, they didn't answer. It's late in New York. I'll call in the morning."

"Or try one of them at home," Cassandra offered.

Jared looked at her. "Good idea. See if you can find home numbers for any of the partners," Jared directed Helen.

When Helen left, Cassandra rose tentatively, holding out the manila folder to Jared. "You probably don't want to be bothered with this right now, but these are the projections we did for the GlobalNet account. I'm confident they are solid, a bit ambitious but achievable. If anything, we erred on the conservative side."

Jared took the folder and leaned back in his chair. Petite with glossy black hair, Cassandra represented the epitome of the young executive on the rise. She always wore her dark hair in a conservative French braid, tidy, neat, severe. Dark-framed glasses perched on her nose. Irreverently Jared thought they made her look like an owl, trying unsuccessfully to hide her eyes. Large and dark, fringed with long lashes, they were her best feature. Jared idly let his gaze drift down her neat suit, navy blue with a standard white blouse. The perfect businesswoman—all work-oriented with femininity ruthlessly squashed. Just like MaryEllen. Was she as ambitious? As consumed with work?

He took the papers and skimmed the top sheet, but his mind wasn't on the figures. *Twins.* He felt stunned. Could it be possible? Had MaryEllen been pregnant when she left San Francisco? If so, why had she kept the news from him? He couldn't believe it. Yet the attorney's letter seemed clear on the subject.

"We're all sorry about Mrs. Hunter's death," Cassandra said.

Meeting her eyes, Jared stared at her for a long moment. How was he to answer the sentiment? The employees probably expected a grieving husband. No, Helen had said they understood his marriage. He mourned the loss of a close friend, a strong business associate.

Yet now it looked as if he hadn't even known MaryEllen. What was the story with the twins?

"Thank you," he said. What he'd like to do was go home, pour himself a large Scotch and sleep for twelve hours. Instead, he'd wait to see if Helen could reach someone from the New York law office so he could find out what the hell was going on.

"Line one," Helen's voice came on the intercom. "Mr. Randall."

"Jared Hunter here," he said into the phone, motioning Cassandra to sit down again.

"We've been trying to reach you for over a week, Hunter." The speaker had a definite New York twang.

"I believe my secretary explained where I was. The airport just reopened in Bangkok."

"You back in the States?"

"As of a couple of hours ago. I arrived at the office and found your letter. What kind of scam is this?" As far as Jared was concerned, it was just that unless proved otherwise.

"No scam, Hunter. Ashley and Brittany Hunter are your daughters, twins. Cute as can be, too."

"I never heard about them." He glanced at Cassandra, noticing her downcast eyes, as if she were trying to efface her existence. Discreet.

There was a hesitation on the other end of the line. "I am aware of that. Apparently Mrs. Hunter was concerned that you would insist on someone else being in charge of the New York office if you discovered the truth. She, er, enjoyed the business aspect of things— apparently had no inclination to give it up for full-time motherhood. Not that she wasn't a fine mother."

Sounded like lawyer talk—covering all bases, Jared thought. He closed his eyes. MaryEllen had been right. He would have moved heaven and earth to keep her in San Francisco if he'd known she was pregnant. And probably demanded she curtail some of her activities at the office. A mother's place was with her children.

"How old are they?" Jared asked, a sinking feeling in his gut. Could they truly be his? Had MaryEllen hidden that from him just to make sure she could keep forging ahead in the business world? Given her unrelenting determination, he could easily imagine her doing just that.

"Two. A month or so over, maybe. I have the file at

the office. I can look up their birth date in the morning, if you like. Mrs. Hunter made it clear that they were yours and she had not told you of their birth. We thought you would be here for the funeral and the reading of the will. Actually, we haven't read the will yet. Two-year-olds don't understand much, and she left everything she had to them, with you as trustee. We can go over all that when you get here.''

"And where are the twins now?" Jared asked, the enormity of the situation gradually sinking in. *He was a father.* He had two daughters he'd never met who now looked to him for everything. God, he knew nothing about being a parent. He focused on Cassandra, feeling like she was the only solid, real thing in a world suddenly spinning out of control. Her calm demeanor soothed him. Her downcast eyes had him wondering what she was thinking.

"We didn't want them to go into foster care, so one of the receptionists at the office agreed to watch them. She has children of her own and is good with kids. But this has gone on longer than we anticipated."

"I'll see if I can get a red-eye out tonight and be in your office first thing in the morning." Jared hung up the phone.

"I'll call the airlines right away," Helen said from the doorway.

"You heard?" he asked.

"Enough to know you have to get back there. Are the twins yours?"

"Apparently. The age fits. MaryEllen told him they were mine. She left everything to them with me as trustee. Damn! What a mess. I can't believe she didn't tell me."

"Well, I can. Would you have gone along with her

opening a branch office if you had known?'' Helen asked dryly.

Shaking his head, Jared looked at her. ''What do I know about twins? About little kids?'' He rubbed his eyes, his gut churning.

''For one thing, you'll need someone to accompany you,'' Cassandra said. She knew a lot about children, more than she wanted. ''Toddlers are a handful. An inexperienced person would be hard-pressed to manage one on a plane—much less twins. Those little girls will be upset with all the changes, and probably missing their mother, which could make them even more fretful.''

Both Jared and Helen stared at her.

''I assumed you would be bringing them home with you,'' Cassandra said, looking from one to the other.

''If they're mine, I'll have no choice.''

Cassandra nodded. Twins. She smiled gently. She remembered the little boys she'd cared for when she'd been sixteen. What imps they'd been. Whether from being twins or being normal rambunctious boys, she never knew. But they sure kept her busy.

''Any other words of wisdom?'' Jared asked.

She gave a small shrug. ''I've been around kids. If you haven't, you might not know what to expect.''

Jared couldn't believe it. This epitome of a career-track businesswoman around kids? She wasn't married, was she? He tried to remember the interview two years ago. He had been more interested in her credentials than her marital status. But he was certain she was single. ''When were you around kids, in another life?''

She nodded. A life she had hoped to leave behind once she graduated from college. The past two years had been great, no children demanding attention or to fall for and then have to give up. She had her way to make in the world and relished her position at Hunter Associates. Children didn't figure in her plans.

"She's right, Jared. You will need help. You would with even a single child," Helen said. "I'll see if I can find someone to go with you. You'll need to hire a nanny or housekeeper, though it's quite late to get anyone on such short notice."

"Do the best you can. And see what kind of nonstop flight you can get to New York tonight."

Cassandra rose. "Do you want to hear my recommendations on GlobalNet while you're waiting? I could get started on some of the ideas while you're in New York, if you approve."

Business first, last and always, Jared thought tightly. Just like MaryEllen. "Show me what you have." He spread out the computer printout and began to read.

Forty-five minutes later Jared leaned back. He rubbed his eyes with forefinger and thumb, then stretched to get rid of the kinks in his back. That Scotch sounded better and better.

The work Cassandra had done was solid, just as she'd said. Interestingly, she gave credit to the entire team she headed, but he knew everyone acted under her direction. She was good at her job—he'd suspected she would be when he hired her two years ago, nearly a year after MaryEllen had moved to New York.

"So we go?" she asked, a tremor of excitement in her voice, a hint of anticipation in her eyes.

"We go. Good job." He believed in giving praise where it was due.

She smiled. Jared felt the jolt to his toes. Her face seemed to glow with the offhand praise. Her eyes sparkled, and for the first time he wondered what she would look like without her glasses. What would she look like with her hair down, swirling softly around her face? What would she look like wearing something frilly and feminine? Before he could pursue the image, Helen stuck her head in.

"Got you two seats on the eleven-thirty flight tonight. But no help as of yet. Every agency I called said they'd look into it. One called back with a possible for next week. Nothing for today. And they're closing now, so I don't expect any answers before tomorrow."

"So what next?" Jared murmured, his eyes closed. He longed for that Scotch more than ever. Maybe he'd have time to get home, shower and have one before he had to leave for the airport. How much work did he absolutely have to get through before leaving? His employees were competent. He could delegate everything until he returned from New York. The looming problem with the twins overshadowed the normal business routine.

"Maybe Cassandra can go with you. She said she knows kids," Helen suggested.

"What?" Cassandra shook her head, a look of sheer horror on her face. "No way. I swore once I grew up I would never get involved baby-sitting children again. I don't want to spend even an hour watching other people's kids!"

Jared and Helen stared at her vehemence. She took a deep breath, knowing she'd overreacted. But she was adamant—she had watched her last child. She was a businesswoman. Hadn't Jared just praised her work? Given her the go-ahead on the GlobalNet project? She had better things to do than baby-sit the boss's children.

"You wouldn't be watching them, precisely," Helen said placatingly. "Just helping Jared with them on the return flight. He needs your expertise."

Cassandra shook her head. The old feeling of helplessness began to rise. Why did everyone expect her to be the nurturer? What about her *own* needs? When would someone look to see what *she* wanted, needed, to feel complete? To feel valued? She was more than a competent baby-sitter—and had the degrees to prove it.

Jared narrowed his eyes. "Sounds like the best suggestion I've heard so far. It'll just be a short jaunt to New York. We'll discuss GlobalNet on the flight over. You can give me pointers on watching twins on the flight back. Consider it part of your job."

"It's not part of my job." Cassandra faced him, her hands fisted in her lap. She dare not cross the line with her boss, but she had to stand up for herself. She didn't want to be thought of as a baby-sitter just because she was a woman.

For a moment Jared was struck by the sparkle in her dark eyes, the challenging tilt of her rounded chin. Slowly he said, "There's a clause in your job description that includes other tasks as assigned. I need help, doesn't look like anyone else is available. As of now, consider this as another task assigned."

"You're his secretary, can't you go?" Cassandra turned to Helen, her plea obvious.

"Afraid not. I have an invalid mother I care for. I can't leave her alone overnight. Besides, I don't know any more about children than Jared."

"I was hired as a marketing analyst, not a nanny," Cassandra protested, swinging to Jared.

He smiled sardonically, anger edging him. "I believe in utilizing all experiences of my employees. Consider yourself indispensable for this assignment."

"I protest." She said it firmly, yet deep inside she knew it wouldn't matter. Jared wasn't listening.

"It's settled. Meet me at the airport in time for the flight. Helen, give her the details. I'm heading home." He caught her eye and narrowed his. "Don't be late!"

Cassandra watched him leave, the unfairness of it all striking her. She met the sympathy in Helen's gaze.

"He needs your help. You said you know something about kids, he hasn't a clue. It's just overnight, Cassandra," the older woman said.

"I'm always the one stuck with children. For years, it was always, 'Leave them with Cassandra'. Working here was my chance to leave that behind," she said wryly, rising. "Guess that was wishful thinking." She took a deep breath. Trying to look on the bright side of things, she wandered to her desk. Casting her mind back, she tried to picture the needs and abilities of toddlers. It really hadn't been that long since she'd been in charge of little children. She could certainly handle a cross-country flight.

And she'd have Jared's attention on the flight to New York. Maybe she could discuss some of her other ideas with him. Looking for the silver lining, she swept folders into her briefcase and headed home to pack.

Four hours later Jared leaned back on his sofa watching the clock on the mantel. In ten minutes he had to leave for the airport. He'd had a Scotch, but it had done nothing to ease the turmoil. Sleeping had been out of the question—he'd been afraid he wouldn't wake up in time for the flight. He'd sleep on the plane. It would have to do. He considered the situation once again, trying to make some sense of it.

Oddly, his thoughts kept returning to Cassandra Bowles. For the two years she'd worked for him, he'd barely noticed her. She'd done her job well, already had one promotion behind her. Recently she'd been assigned as project manager for the GlobalNet account. Accomplished, proficient, professional—all desirable attributes for a career-minded woman. Her surprising outburst this afternoon startled him. Jared liked things to make sense, to follow a logical pattern—and that hadn't. She was usually enthusiastic and agreeable, and her refusal had been surprising and unusual. A mere suggestion to accompany him on the trip to see to the children, help bring them to San Francisco, and she'd just about exploded. He wondered why.

Maybe he'd discover on the trip.

The red-eye flight would arrive in New York just after eight. They'd go directly to the attorney's office upon landing. Jared had showered and shaved, donned a fresh suit and shirt. His overnight case contained casual clothes for the return journey. He might not know much about children, but he knew enough to suspect they'd be too messy for an Armani suit.

He wondered what he should be taking to entertain two toddlers.

His thoughts veered to the babies. How could MaryEllen have kept them a secret? If her lawyer was to be believed, she feared he would demand she return to San Francisco. Would that have been so bad? They'd worked together at McGeorge and Fergarson, discussed starting a business for months before taking the plunge. She'd had as much invested in the company as he. Pouring all their resources into the firm, they'd conserved on expenses by marrying each other. He liked the challenge of building a company, but sometimes he thought MaryEllen defined herself by the company and its success. Had business been more important to her than her children?

He rose, not liking the trend of his thoughts. He grabbed the overnight case and started for the airport.

Cassandra sat alone in a bank of chairs at the boarding gate, casually reading a magazine, a small tote bag beside her feet. She might resent the assignment, but she was professional enough to do her best. Knowing they'd head directly for the attorney's offices, she'd dressed in a charcoal gray suit matched with a white blouse. Both traveled well, and she hoped she wouldn't look like a wrinkled mess in the morning. A tingling awareness struck her, and she raised her gaze. As if attuned to him, she spotted her boss as he crossed the concourse toward the gate.

She sighed softly and sat up straighter. Jared was so good-looking he shouldn't be let out without a keeper. Unconsciously she noticed the glances he received from the other women in the area. Some bold and interested, others more surreptitious, but all following his long stride as he crossed to join her. His dark hair was thick and neatly trimmed. The tan he'd had in the summer was not as evident after his recent trip, but the rugged masculinity in his face struck a spark of interest for the first time.

Cassandra frowned. Was it knowing he was single again that caused that? She'd thought he was drop-dead gorgeous when he'd interviewed her, but so far out of her league, she'd immediately ignored the sensations that flittered inside her and concentrated on doing the best she could on her assignment.

In reality, nothing had changed. So why this sudden awareness? She smiled politely as he drew closer.

"Here as ordered, sir," she said briefly.

He sat beside her and glanced at her carryon bag and

briefcase. A sardonic smile creased his cheeks. "You sound like a kitten spitting at a bulldog. Just remember who's the boss."

She met his hard eyes, a faint hint of anger visible in her gaze. "No danger of forgetting that, is there?"

Jared smiled.

She tightened her lips and returned to her magazine before she gave way to the urge to slap that smug grin off his face.

"Do you sleep in suits?" he asked.

"What?" She looked around and stared at him in disbelief.

"Just wondering. MaryEllen wore suits all the time except to bed. I thought you might wear something more comfortable for the flight."

"This is appropriate attire for a business meeting. We *are* meeting the lawyers before we see your daughters, right?" she replied.

"Maybe they'll be dressed like miniature businesswomen, too," he murmured, not putting it past MaryEllen. Wearily Jared felt as if he'd never known his wife at all.

"I doubt it." She eyed his suit. "I hope *you* brought something else. Kids can be messy, especially when confined in airplanes."

He looked at her lazily. "I have a couple of changes in the bag. I figured we would stay at least one night in New York. If I don't get some sleep soon, I'm going to just pass out." He rubbed his eyes with his thumb and forefinger.

"You can sleep on the plane." Compassion struck Cassandra. He did look exhausted. After flying in from Asia, it had to be next to impossible to fly on to New York.

"I'll have to. After the flight from Bangkok and the flight tonight, my body won't know whether it's coming or going. Do you know how many time zones I've crossed in the last twenty-four hours?"

She shook her head, her gaze moving slowly over his shoulders to the long legs stretched out before him. So much for her idea of discussing business on the flight to New York. For a moment Cassandra wondered what it would be like to travel with him when he was rested. Would he be a fascinating conversationalist? He'd been to so many places and done so much. Wasn't he only in his early thirties? She would love to hear how he and his wife had started Hunter Associates and where they planned to take the company.

But it wasn't going to happen tonight, she knew that.

Jared idly noted Cassandra's perusal. Or was he imagining it? She probably wanted to discuss the bottom line or future projections and was trying to think up the best approach. She was no more interested in him than he was in her.

And he was not interested in any woman. Except he couldn't quite explain the desire to loosen her dark hair, unbutton that high collar and remove the glasses. He couldn't remember if he'd ever seen her not wearing them. He wouldn't mind seeing her in a dress, or shorts—or nothing at all.

Nothing?

God, he must be tired—now he was hallucinating. Closing his eyes, he tried to focus on the impending meeting with his daughters. Disbelief warred with fascination. He had no time for idle fantasies about one of his employees—one, moreover, who reminded him strongly of his late wife. He'd had his fill of determined career women who cared more for competing in the business world than in making a home and planning a future complete with family.

Next time he ventured into a personal relationship, he'd find someone soft and feminine and more interested in flowers in the garden and a comfortable home than spreadsheets and bank statements. That's what he'd look for—if he ever wanted to marry again.

The flight was called. Jared and Cassandra boarded first class. He offered her the window seat. "I plan to sleep the entire trip, don't need to see out the window," he said.

"Thank you. Though I should mention I'll also be napping. If not, I'll be a zombie tomorrow." She slipped in, stowed her bag and briefcase, clutched her magazine like a lifeline. Bemused, Cassandra realized she could smell his after-shave lotion—tangy and masculine. Sitting close enough to feel the heat from his strong body, she wanted to draw away, but there was only the airplane wall on the other side. Tongue-tied and feeling awkward, she gazed at the magazine, wondering why all her common sense seemed to have gone cockeyed. Jared sat beside her, fastening his seat belt. She'd attended meetings in the conference room that he'd chaired. So what was the problem tonight?

Of course, at the meetings, she had not sat beside him. Not been so acutely aware of his strong hands, the width of his shoulders and the smooth skin of his freshly shaved jaw. She tightened her grip lest her fingers give way to the desire to brush against that stubborn jaw and test the texture of his skin, feel his heat sear into her.

Cassandra swallowed hard, moving her gaze out the window. There was little to see in the darkness. Lights lit the service vehicles scurrying around the big jetliner, but beyond that nothing was visible. Yet she continued to stare out the window. It felt safer, somehow.

"As soon as we get airborne, I'm reclining the seat and going to sleep. If anyone asks, I don't want food or drink," he murmured in her right ear.

Cassandra turned and drew in her breath. His face was mere inches from hers. She could see the lines of fatigue radiating from his eyes and her own image reflected there. His breath caressed her cheek. Swallowing, she nodded, fascinated to be so close to the man.

"Been to New York before?" he asked, his eyes searching hers.

She shook her head, conscious of the wild beat of her heart. Mesmerized by the sensations that raced through her, she couldn't look away.

"Sorry we won't have time to go sight-seeing."

"I hope to go one day on vacation. I'd like to see the sights, maybe go to a Broadway show."

"It's okay to visit, but I prefer San Francisco any day."

Cassandra nodded.

"Are you from the Bay Area?" he asked.

She shook her head. Feeling like an idiot and not the competent woman she tried to portray, she cleared her throat. "I grew up near L.A. Now I prefer San Francisco."

"Live in the city?"

"In a small place on Telegraph Hill."

"Lots of tourists."

"Mostly in the summer. Coit Tower is a popular site. I like to walk up there myself and gaze out over the city. It offers a magnificent view."

"How long have you lived there?" Jared asked, won-

dering why he didn't know more about an employee who
had worked for him for two years.

"I arrived a couple of weeks before I went to work
for you," she replied. Why didn't he lean back in his
chair? Why was he still so close, close enough for her
to feel as if there were only the two of them on the entire
plane? She longed for some distance. His eyes were
dark, compelling, mesmerizing. She liked the lights that
danced in their depth. Wondered what he thought as he
gazed into her eyes.

The flight attendant began her preflight demonstration.
Cassandra drew a deep breath and looked at the woman.
She knew Jared continued to watch her through narrowed eyes, but she focused on the demonstration as if
she'd never seen one before. Almost feeling the waves
of fatigue wash through him, she knew he'd last only a
few more minutes. Once he reclined his seat and slept,
the trip would be easier.

Jared awoke as the plane began its descent. He felt the
pressure in his ears and yawned to relieve it. Something
heavy and warm rested against his shoulder. Turning his
head, he realized Cassandra had decided to use him as
a pillow during the night. Both of them were covered
with airline blankets. Both seats had been reclined. Had
he done this? Had she?

He shifted a bit, his arm asleep. How long had she
rested against him? A faint hint of roses wafted on the
air. Her special scent? He tipped his face toward her and
took a breath. Sweet, definitely roses. Closing his eyes,
he tried to envision her purchasing that particular scent
and spraying it on each morning. Somehow it evoked
images of a different woman, soft and feminine—not a
straitlaced, ambitious businesswoman.

He had to get a grip. She was not there to be his personal fantasy, but to play nanny to his daughters on the return trip. That was all. Once they reached San Francisco, she'd resume her role as marketing analyst, and Helen would have located a nanny for the twins. He had other things to think about besides Cassandra Bowles.

Immediately thoughts of the twins had him awake and alert.

He shook his seat companion, then waited while she slowly came awake.

"Oh, sorry." Instantly she pushed back and sat up. Her cheek was warm and rosy, with a slight crease mark from his jacket crossing it diagonally. She looked at him and blinked. The glasses were gone. Her eyes were dark and mysterious. Slowly Jared felt attraction build. Glasses off, she looked younger, shy almost, and definitely as feminine as he could ever wish. Her tight French braid had worked loose during the night. Wispy tendrils of glossy dark hair framed her face. When she licked dry lips, he felt a sharp tug of awareness—total male awareness of an attractive female. All thoughts of sleep fled. Suddenly he was more than curious about this woman.

"I didn't mean to fall asleep on you," she said, moving farther away, straightening her clothes beneath the blanket, retrieving her glasses. Jared experienced a repeat urge to unbutton the top of her blouse to enable more of her warmth and sweet scent to fill his senses. He looked at her moist lips and yearned to taste her.

Closing his eyes, he turned away. He'd been too long without a woman. Even in a business marriage, he'd believed in keeping his vows. Since MaryEllen had departed almost three years ago, he'd spent his nights alone. Sexual deprivation—that was all it was. And now that his wife was dead, he was free to consider other women. Nothing more than that. He was not attracted to Cassandra. Any woman would affect him the same way.

Opening his eyes, he didn't bother to analyze why there was no pull of attraction between him and the buxom blond flight attendant. Instead, he tried to ignore the attraction to the woman beside him and concentrate on attempting to anticipate the information he'd receive from the attorney.

When they landed, Jared reached for Cassandra's cases and carried them easily.

"I can manage my own cases," she protested, following him up the jetway.

"I don't mind. You'll have your hands full later. No sense in not taking advantage of my generous nature now."

"Generous, my foot," she mumbled. "Dictatorial, more likely."

"Why's that?" Jared found himself amused at her grumbling. Was she always cranky in the morning? For the first time her perfect image shifted, blurred. He liked her better when she wasn't the flawless employee.

"You ordered me here. I didn't want to come."

"Don't you like children?"

"I don't like watching them."

"When was the last time you did?"

Kennedy Airport hummed with activity. A uniformed man stood in the crowd holding Jared's name on a card. Jared handed the limousine driver the bags. Following him, Jared placed his hand on Cassandra's back. She was not as tall as MaryEllen had been. Yet she held her head high and marched determinedly after the driver.

"Children?" Jared said again, a hint of steel in his voice.

"I've had to watch children almost all my life. I swore when I was on my own I wouldn't do it again. I'm not real happy with this assignment. If you hadn't made it an order, I wouldn't be here," she grumbled. Despite her annoyance with her high-handed boss, she was fascinated with the bustle of the international airport.

"Ah, but think of the brownie points you can rack up helping the boss out this way."

"I'd rather get points for merit than for baby-sitting capability."

"Maybe the merit is in the baby-sitting," he replied calmly, noting her agitation. "Tell me about watching kids all your life."

"I'd rather not. I'm sorry I opened my mouth yesterday."

"About knowing about twins?"

She nodded. Dodging a man obviously in a hurry to make a plane, she pushed against Jared. He shifted her to the other side, continued walking smoothly.

"It slipped out," she said.

More curious than ever, Jared wondered if he could get the full story from her before they met with MaryEllen's attorneys.

CHAPTER TWO

"I HAVE to compliment you on your restraint and tact,"
Jared said to Cassandra when they were seated in the
back of the limousine heading for Manhattan.

"About what?" she asked warily.

After entering the limousine, Cassandra had moved as
close to the far door as possible. Jared almost smiled at
the distance she placed between them. Was she uncomfortable around him? Interesting. For a moment he considered testing the theory.

"Another woman would have bombarded me with
questions about my marriage, my wife and why I apparently have two-year-old daughters I know nothing
about," he said instead.

"Of course I'm curious, but I do respect your right to
privacy." She tilted her head and smiled mischievously.
"And I picked up quite a bit from around the office. The
scuttlebutt is that you two married to pool resources so
you could build Hunter Associates. She moved to New
York a few years ago to open a second office and to try
to crack the European market. She had two little girls
you knew nothing about. If there's more you want to
volunteer, I wouldn't interrupt."

Startled, Jared almost laughed aloud at the unexpected
glimpse of minx in his companion. He knew what she
had told him was no secret—except for the babies. He
was more intrigued that she had apparently picked up
quite a bit. Any special reason?

"Ours was not an ordinary marriage. We married for

expediency. Starting up a new company calls for a lot of hard work, long hours and money. It was easier to minimize expenses and to work long hours by sharing a home.'' He wasn't trying to justify the relationship, just explain it. Why that was important, he wasn't sure.

"Sounds like a business arrangement."

"Essentially." He had almost forgotten how it started. For the last three years they had shared nothing beyond a meal in Washington. "MaryEllen wanted Hunter Associates to succeed even more than I did. She found the business environment challenging and exciting.''

"It can be exhilarating," Cassandra murmured, watching ing him closely.

"I know. Now I understand her sudden determination to move to New York and open an East Coast office. She never came back to San Francisco because she feared she'd be stuck with the babies rather than in the trenches of high-tech business, I think.''

"Not every woman wants to stay home and raise children.''

"You don't," he stated with certainty. Her outburst yesterday in his office confirmed that.

"What I want right now is a chance to build a life of my own. Maybe down the road I'll marry and have children. Then I'll have to see what I want to do. Children are fine as long as they are wanted and loved.''

"I hear a but."

"But I don't want the choice taken from me."

"As I did with this assignment?''

She nodded, looking out the window as the tall skyscrapers of Manhattan came into view. Puffy white clouds drifted in azure blue skies. Traffic was heavy, but moving steadily on the congested highway. Jared wondered if her attention was truly taken with the approaching city or if she was trying to distance herself to rebuild her anger. It had blown over quickly. He was glad she wasn't the type to sulk.

"Be honest, Cassandra. I didn't ask for much. A day to help get them home. Helen is working on finding a nanny. You have experience I lack. Wouldn't you take advantage of any needed expertise?"

"Probably," she admitted grudgingly.

"Where does that expertise come from? Lots of brothers and sisters?" He knew he was probing where she didn't want him to, but his curiosity rose. Solemn and serious, Cassandra Bowles never gave the impression she was anything but a well-trained employee. Yet she had to have a private life—he didn't demand his employees dedicate their entire waking hours to the job. Suddenly he wanted to know more.

"None, actually."

"We have about thirty minutes before we arrive at the attorneys' office. Why don't you tell me about your experience with children." If she wouldn't open up voluntarily, he'd ask specific questions. For a moment he wondered why he pushed. Was it only curiosity, or was he trying to stop thinking about two toddlers waiting to meet him? He'd negotiated multimillion-dollar deals. Why was he growing more and more nervous at the thought of facing two small girls?

The silence stretched. Cassandra slowly turned and looked at him assessingly. She didn't like to talk about her past. All her life she'd wished for a fairy-tale family, something like the Brady Bunch—a dream far from her reality. She guessed it wouldn't hurt to explain why she hadn't wanted to come on this trip.

"My mother died when I was seven. I had no other family, so I ended up in foster care. The home I was assigned when I was ten had lots of young children, mostly other foster kids. I baby-sat constantly over the next eight years. Once I turned eighteen, I split. No more kids for me, I vowed.''

''Until today.''

''I wish. When I got to college, I needed money. Only job I was qualified for was watching children. So I was a prime candidate for professors' families looking for baby-sitters. Another four years of watching other people's kids.''

''Now mine.''

''Right.'' She frowned. ''It's not what I expected when I hired on with the firm. I have a degree in marketing, not child care. I want to use my mind, not be a baby-sitter.''

''Nor did I ever think I'd need a baby-sitter. But then I had no idea MaryEllen had delivered twins.'' Jared lapsed into silence, again wondering how MaryEllen could have kept such an event from him. After all, he couldn't have made her return to San Francisco to live. He *should* have known about his daughters.

The law offices of Sattler, Randall and Peabody were located on the thirty-third floor of a skyscraper on East Fortieth Street. A high-speed elevator whisked them quickly to their destination. Jared located the door to the offices, pushed it open and stood aside to allow Cassandra to enter. Stepping inside, he immediately stopped, his eyes on the two toddlers playing by a maroon-colored crushed velvet sofa. Dark hair caught up in wispy ponytails, matching overalls, a pink shirt and a yellow shirt on the two little girls—other than those shirts, they were identical. Both stopped playing when

Jared entered, turning toward him and Cassandra, bright blue eyes staring.

Jared stood more than six feet tall. Did he seem like a giant to these little creatures? They were so tiny. For an instant he stared in fascination, wondering what they thought. Neither said a word, just stared.

"Hello, there." Cassandra greeted the little girls and moved closer. They were precious. Her heart went out to them. Things must be so scary. Cassandra remembered how scared she'd been when her mother died and she had gone to live with strangers. Nothing had been familiar, nothing comforting. And she'd missed her mother so much.

Smiling, she knelt before the girls and slowly reached out to touch each one on her hand. "Hi, I'm Cassie. What are your names?"

Jared heard the warmth and softness in her voice. It broke the spell. The twins smiled and shifted their gaze to Cassandra. When she knelt before them, they launched into babbling that had Jared's head spinning. Would she understand anything they were saying? He'd forgotten how small two-year-olds were. They didn't even talk well.

"Mr. Hunter?" The woman behind the reception desk greeted him. Her smile was friendly.

"That's right."

"Cute kids you have," she said with a glance at the twins. "I've been watching them for the last two weeks. They're as sweet as can be. I'm so sorry about your wife."

Jared nodded, feeling totally out of his element. He knew nothing about children—knew nothing about his own daughters! Fortunately, Cassandra appeared to know all that was needed. The twins took to her like ducks to water. Laughing and talking, the three of them, all the same height with Cassandra kneeling, seemed to mesh perfectly. For a moment Jared was envious. He watched them while the receptionist notified the attorney of Jared's arrival.

"Mr. Randall will be with you in just a moment," the receptionist said, seemingly unaware of his hesitation.

Nodding, Jared moved slowly across the reception area toward his children. One look at them and all doubts fled. They looked just like he had as a child—though feminine versions. He could see nothing of MaryEllen in either child except for her blue eyes. Had they inherited her temperament or ambition?

"Hello," he said.

Two pairs of identical eyes swiveled to him. The little girl in yellow put her thumb in her mouth, watching him warily.

"I think you are a bit too tall for them. Either pick them up, or get down on their level," Cassandra suggested, leaning on her heels. She brushed the hair off the face of the child sucking her thumb.

Jared stared at the unwavering eyes regarding him. Slowly he sat on the edge of the sofa, totally at a loss. He didn't like the feeling. Over the years, he'd perfected his ability to fit in with different cultures, different societies as he expanded Hunter Associates in Pacific Rim countries. Now he was floored by a pair of babies.

"Smile," Cassandra said, the lilt in her voice one of amusement. "This is your daddy. Tell him your name," she prompted the twin in pink.

"Asslee," she said proudly, her gaze steady.

Popping her thumb from her mouth, the other twin piped up. "Me Bitnee."

"Ashley and Brittany," Cassandra repeated, smiling at them. "And this is your daddy. Can you say Daddy?"

For a moment Jared was struck by the change on her face. He wished she would smile at him like that. For the first time he realized how lucky he was that she had responded when he'd yelled for Helen yesterday. He couldn't have handled these children by himself. They stood by Cassandra, shaking their heads. Then Ashley began talking nineteen to the dozen. Cassandra listened as if she understood every word, nodding and smiling. Maybe she did. But he didn't.

A father should be better able to cope. What was he going to do? Dealing on an international level in business was one thing. The thought of dealing with these toddlers scared him half to death.

Cassandra stayed in the reception area with the twins when Jared met with MaryEllen's attorney, Thomas Randall. The girls had warmed up to her, and she thought it best to have as few disruptions as possible. They already had experienced a lot of change. She would try to make things easier for them.

Sitting on the sofa, she enticed them to sit beside her, one on each side. "Let me tell you a story. It's about two big girls who just met their daddy..." Trying to explain the coming changes in a story, Cassandra told the tale in simple terms. She made flying sound like a grand adventure and moving to San Francisco as normal as brushing their teeth.

When Thomas Randall offered to read the will aloud, Jared asked if he could skim it himself. It took only a few minutes. The will was short and simple. The half interest MaryEllen owned in the company was left in trust to her daughters, to be administered by her husband, the children's father. Jared looked at the attorney when he finished.

"She was a young woman. Her death caught me by surprise," Jared said. He wondered how much the man knew about their marriage.

The attorney nodded. "The children's baby-sitter called us when MaryEllen went into the hospital. I went to see your wife just before she died. She was very sick. I think she pushed herself too hard and had no reserves when the end came."

"The girls will miss her," Jared murmured.

"Not as much as you might suspect," Randall said. "Apparently there have been a series of baby-sitters and housekeepers over the last couple of years. I don't believe the girls are strongly attached to anyone—even their mother. My receptionist reported they adjusted well to staying with her."

"I'll get them established in a stable environment. I have to return to San Francisco," Jared said.

"We expected that. I have all the paperwork right here. Anything else we can do, just ask."

"I'd like directions to the cemetery," Jared said as he began to read the legal papers that would wind up MaryEllen's estate.

When Jared finished with the lawyer, he returned to the reception area where Cassandra sat on the sofa softly reading aloud, a twin snuggled on each side, their eyes on the pages of the book. For a moment they didn't see him. He took the time to study the group, aware of a curious yearning. *That is what a family would look like. A mother devoted to her children, all of them waiting for the father.*

He hadn't realized before that he had no clear vision of a family. He'd been raised by his grandfather, a gruff old man. There'd been few amenities or social graces in that all-male household, but at least he had had his grandfather when his parents had died. He had not gone into foster care like Cassandra. Nor would his children!

His goal for the last decade had been to establish his company, make it a success. He'd never given a thought to starting a family. Now he'd been presented with a ready-made one. Was the next step to acquire another wife?

One of the twins looked up, the one who sucked her thumb. Brittany?

"Man," she said.

Cassandra looked up. "How'd it go?"

"Fine. I'm finished here. We can head for MaryEllen's apartment. We'll need to pack the children's clothes and toys. I'll also have to get an idea of what's needed to close the place. Later I want to swing by the office and make sure things are settled there. Paul will be in charge. I want to review the current projects with him."

For a moment he thought her lips tightened, and he remembered her comment about having kids dumped on her. But it couldn't be helped. No matter her likes or dislikes, Cassandra looked like a natural with those twins, and he hadn't a clue how to begin. It was only for a day. Then she'd be back in the office and could stay away from children for the rest of her life if she so chose.

"As long as you realize you have to pull your own weight," she said, disengaging herself and rising. "Come on, munchkins, time to go home. Brittany, you come with me. Ashley, you go with Daddy."

He almost didn't recognize the appellation. He was the *daddy* of these children.

Cassandra picked up Brittany and propped her on her hip. She looked at Jared, her dark, solemn eyes behind her glasses. Was there a hint of a challenge in her gaze?

Jared reached down and picked up Ashley. She was light as a feather. Holding her against his chest, he stared into her eyes. She patted his cheek and smiled. Something tugged in his heart. She was precious. Small and alone and totally dependent upon him to care for her. Panic nipped at his heels. Could he do it? What if he screwed up? He knew nothing about parenting. Had thought to work up to it, if ever he'd decided to take the plunge. Read books while his wife was pregnant, learn as they went along. Not be an instant father with no warning and no time to prepare.

"Let's go, Daddy." Amusement danced in Cassandra's eyes, but she kept the smile from her lips. No point in letting Jared know she found his uncertainty touching. He was a dynamo in the office. Now he looked as awkward as a teenager on a first date. She blinked and led the way from the reception area. Why in the world had she thought about dating? She was a baby-sitter, that's all. He was dumping his children on her and taking off for the New York office, abdicating all responsibility for a day. Sometimes it didn't pay to open your mouth!

Adding the small bag for the twins to the others, he followed. Cassandra waited by the elevator, allowing Brittany to press the buttons. Both were lit, but she didn't care. They'd just wait for a down elevator. Children liked to experiment and try things. She may be mad at their father for insisting she accompany him, but she would never take that anger out on these children.

MaryEllen Hunter's apartment came as a surprise. It was large, formally decorated in delicate Queen Anne furnishings and located in a prestigious neighborhood only two blocks from Central Park. When they entered, Jared placed Ashley on the floor. She didn't move. Cassandra deposited Brittany beside her. The two girls looked at the adults.

"Where's your room?" Cassandra asked.

Ashley pointed down the hall.

Crossing into the living room, Jared dropped their bags on the floor beside an ornate credenza that took up most of the wall. Surveying the room, he wondered when MaryEllen had decided to go for the elegant look. Their place in San Francisco had been comfortable with sturdy furniture and few knickknacks. Maybe this style fit with her idea of living in New York. He didn't like it much, but he was more interested in comfort at home.

"No, no," Brittany said when Cassandra started to follow.

"What?"

"No, no." Brittany shook her head, warily eyeing the living room.

The phone rang.

Jared crossed to answer it, puzzled by Brittany.

"Jared Hunter."

"Mr. Hunter, this is Annie Simmons. Mr. Randall called a little while ago and suggested I get in touch with you. I was the twins' baby-sitter. The most recent one, I should say. I understand you'll be taking the children back to San Francisco with you, but if I can help in the meantime, please let me know. I don't start another job for a week."

"We plan to leave tomorrow." Jared glanced at Cassandra. "But if you could come by today, that would be great. You could help us pack their things, maybe suggest where I can dispose of what we don't take with us.''

''Surely. I could stop by around one.''

Jared checked his watch. It wasn't even noon. ''That will be fine.''

''I'll be there.''

Cassandra and the twins had disappeared. He followed the sound of voices drifting down the hall and stopped at the door to their bedroom. It was large, with two cribs, a highboy dresser and more dolls and stuffed animals scattered around than most toy stores carried. MaryEllen hadn't stinted on gifts for her daughters.

Brittany stood near the wall, watching Cassandra and Ashley, thumb firmly in her mouth. He wondered why one sucked her thumb and the other didn't. Of course in the short drive from the attorney's office, he'd noticed the difference in the personalities of the two. Ashley was outgoing and friendly. Curious and fearless. Brittany seemed to watch carefully, shy and quiet. Interesting with identical twins. Or was that the norm? He had so much to learn.

''That was the girls' baby-sitter. She'll stop by at one to help pack.''

Cassandra nodded, took off her suit jacket and tossed it across the rails of one of the cribs. The soft material of her blouse draped over her trim figure, Jared noticed. His eyes skimmed over her curves. Again he wondered what she would look like in lacy, frilly dresses. It was probably something he'd never see. She was an employee, here under protest to help him with his newly discovered daughters. Nothing else.

He shook his head. Who was he kidding? Only himself. Because he was the only one who knew about the attraction he felt around Cassandra Bowles. And it had better stay that way. A passing fancy. Once he caught up on sleep, got into the routine of work, he'd move beyond any such awareness.

Or so he hoped.

"If you find the suitcases, I'll start packing," Cassandra said, opening a drawer in the high dresser. Might as well make the most of the situation. She could get started on packing, then sort favorite toys and books when the baby-sitter arrived. She'd also make sure she found out as much as she could about the twins' habits, likes and dislikes. Poor babies needed all the help they could get, moving to an entirely new life-style. She glanced at Jared, startled to find his gaze traveling over her body. Heat flushed through her. Swallowing hard, she shifted and turned her back. The unexpected tingling was not a sensation she'd felt before. She wasn't getting sick, was she? No, it was the constant state of awareness she felt around Jared Hunter.

Clearing her throat, she thought longingly about her bag. She had jeans and a shirt in it. Maybe she should change before she did anything else.

"It may take me a while to find them." Jared went into the hallway and entered the second bedroom.

Find what? Oh, the suitcases for the children. Cassandra pressed her hands against her cheeks, feeling the heat. She was acting like an idiot. She was here to take care of his children, nothing else. And she had better remember that every minute!

She trailed after Jared and found him in what must have been his wife's bedroom. MaryEllen's things still lay strewn about. The bed was unmade, as if she'd risen only that morning to head for the hospital. A pang hit her. MaryEllen had been alone at the end. If his trip to

Bangkok had been postponed, if the typhoon hadn't struck, Jared could have been with her.

"I'm sorry you didn't make it back in time," she said softly, watching the bleak look in his eyes.

"I didn't even know she was sick. She should have told me."

"Maybe she didn't think it was serious until too late. Maybe she didn't know how serious."

"I would have insisted the doctors try everything in their power to keep her alive."

"I'm sure they did all they could." She longed to offer comfort, but was unsure what to say. Did he want to talk about it? Knowing human touch could help, she reached out and clasped his hand, squeezing a bit, just to let him know he wasn't alone.

"I don't know a thing about taking care of babies," he said, looking around the room. But the tight grip of his hand let Cassandra know he didn't want to be alone.

"You'll learn what you need to know. And you can afford competent help to take care of a lot of the routine things."

A shriek of laughter came from the twins' room.

"I guess I'd better check on them," Cassandra said, squeezing his hand one last time before she slowly let go. For a moment he held on, then released her.

"I'll hunt up those suitcases."

Jared opened the closet door. Clothes filled the space. In the back, to the left, sat a matching set of expensive leather luggage. He drew the suitcases out, brushing against the clothes. He realized they still carried the faint scent of MaryEllen's perfume. He couldn't believe he wouldn't see her again, wouldn't go toe-to-toe with her over some business decision. Wouldn't hear her wild dreams, most of which had a basic, strong concept they usually implemented. Wouldn't argue about the rate of expansion and the cost-cutting measures he always demanded.

Shaking his head, dispelling memories, Jared returned to the children's room.

"The water is too cold to swim in. When you walk outside it will be windy some days, cool from the bay, but that's good for flying kites." Cassandra chatted with the children as she stacked clothes on one of the cribs.

"What are you telling them?" Jared asked, looking for a place to put the suitcases.

"About their new home. I think they'll feel more comfortable knowing about the change," she said. "Just put them on the floor. There's no room anywhere else."

"Here, Ashley, you put this in the suitcase." Cassandra handed the toddler two folded shirts. Ashley walked to the suitcase and dumped them in.

"Great technique, kid," Jared muttered.

Cassandra laughed. "It doesn't matter. They just want to help," she said as she handed a similar stack to Brittany.

"Why not just dump the drawers into the case if you're not going to have them neatly folded?" he asked, watching the jumble of shirts steadily growing in the suitcase.

"When they nap, I'll fold everything. Right now this keeps them occupied and gives them the feeling they are helping, that they're participating in this move."

"Psychology, too?" He raised an eyebrow, studying her.

"Practical, actually. You could help."

"You've got a system going. I think I'll check out MaryEllen's things. See if I can find her personal papers and pack them. I'll have to get someone in to close up this place."

"Find some things of their mother's that the children can have when they are older," Cassandra suggested. "They won't remember her, poor babies, but it will be nice for them when they're grown to have something of their mother."

He heard the wistful note in her voice.

"Do you?" he asked softly. Knowing he was treading on personal ground, he still had to know.

She shook her head. "That's why I know they'll appreciate it. We had so little. I don't know what happened to our things. Social Services came for me, we packed my clothes, and I got to take one doll. That was all."

"That's tough." He remembered his grandfather's complaining, when his parents died, about having to store furniture and boxes in that shed in the back. Most of it was still there—a link to parents he scarcely remembered.

"It was a long time ago." She smiled at him, her head tilted slightly.

"I'll find a few things for the girls. I could have everything shipped to the West Coast," Jared said, his heart skipping a beat at her smile.

"You're the boss. But they may not want this furniture. Just mementos."

Jared shrugged out of his suit jacket, slung it over one shoulder and headed for the living room. He tossed the jacket on the back of the sofa and looked around. The art on the walls was good quality. The figurines and vases would make nice mementos. Had they held special meaning for MaryEllen, or had she chosen them to complement the decor? Odd he knew so little about a woman to whom he'd been married for so long. He crossed the room, then paused by a small antique desk. The drawers contained MaryEllen's papers—most recent bills, bank statements, address book and other items.

Jared sat down and began to go through everything.

By the time Annie Simmons arrived at one, Jared longed to escape the madhouse of the apartment and find some sort of order at the New York office of Hunter Associates. The girls ran back and forth between Cassandra and him. They'd been hesitant at first to enter the living room, but he'd made it clear they could come to him when they wanted. Laughing, shrieking and running on their sturdy little legs, they displayed more energy than he'd seen in years.

Annie Simmons appeared to be in her mid-forties. The twins greeted her with happy smiles and hugged her, then began talking so fast he hadn't a clue what they were saying. Yet Annie and Cassandra both seemed to understand. Did women come with some sort of built-in translator?

"I'll miss these babies, that's for sure," Annie said after she'd listened to them for a few minutes. "They were so good. I'm sorry, Mr. Hunter, for the loss of your wife."

Jared nodded, feeling that awkwardness again. He wanted to stop by the cemetery on the way to the office. See where she was, if anything else was needed.

"We're hoping you can fill us in on the twins, what they like, what their schedule is. We'll be leaving tomorrow for San Francisco," Cassandra said, giving him an odd look.

"Be glad to tell you all I know. I watched them for five months. Children sure grow fast at this age. I swear they seem even taller than the last time I saw them."

"I'm going to have to get to the office. Cassandra, can you take over here?" Jared asked, anxious to leave.

She nodded. "Of course."

"Are you going to be the twins' new baby-sitter?" Annie asked as Jared pulled the door closed behind him.

"No. I work in the San Francisco offices of Hunter Associates. I just came to help Jared get the children home," Cassandra said quickly. She didn't want anyone, even Annie Simmons, to think her new role in life was nanny to these children. This was a two-day assignment, that was all.

Though for a moment as she watched Ashley run to the window to see if she could see the man leave, she wondered if she could stop by Jared's place once in a while to see them. Frowning, she led the way into the bedroom. She didn't want to form an attachment for these children. She had her future mapped out.

It was after five by the time Jared let himself into the apartment. Cassandra sat on one of the elegant wing chairs near the fireplace, a book opened on her lap. She had changed into her casual clothes—jeans and a soft cotton top. She glanced up when he closed the door.

"Everything all right at the office?" she asked, marking her place in the book with a finger.

Rubbing the back of his neck, Jared nodded. He crossed into the living room and looked around. "Things will settle down there soon. Paul Whitstone will make a good general manager. Where are the twins?" he asked, sinking down in the brocade-covered sofa.

"I put them down for a nap a little while ago. Annie says they nap every afternoon. After the activities of the day, I expect they'll sleep for a while yet. Though we should wake them up before too long, so they'll sleep tonight.''

Loosening his tie, he lay his head against the sofa back. Cassandra watched him, considering how tired he must still be. The short ride on the plane hadn't been enough time to catch up on sleep. And he'd been going full tilt all day.

"Tired?" she asked sympathetically. The entire day must have been a strain, even without the lack of sleep.

"I'd like to go to sleep for a week!"

"Sorry, we leave in the morning.''

"Was Annie Simmons helpful in telling you about the twins?''

"I learned a lot. You should have stayed, however. What if I forget to tell you something or you have questions I didn't think to ask? I did get her phone number, so you can call her if you need to know more—like Ashley throws tantrums if she doesn't get her way, and Brittany runs and hides. Brittany doesn't like eggs. Ashley has a bigger vocabulary. And your wife didn't let the kids in most of the apartment for fear they'd ruin things. That explained their hesitation in entering the living room.''

Jared heard the indignation in her tone. He wanted to smile. She might not like having kids dumped on her, but she stood up for them. Obviously she thought children should have the run of their home. Well, he did, too, as a matter of fact.

"Having been properly chastised, I'd like you to tell me more about these girls. What am I to do with them when I get them home?'' He leaned against the sofa cushions, listening to her voice. It was low and sweet.

"Hope that Helen has found a nanny for you.''

"Think I can't make it as a single father?'' he asked,

curious to hear her reaction. He had his doubts. Did everyone else, as well?

"If today is anything to go by, you'll make a great father. You were quite patient with them, if a bit stiff. They will need a lot of love, attention and guidelines."

"It would be easier if I had a wife."

CHAPTER THREE

CASSANDRA'S eyes met his. For an instant she felt heat steal into her cheeks. She looked away and hoped he hadn't noticed. What would it be like to be married to Jared Hunter? To have him come home every night and discuss his day. To plan family outings for the weekend, to laugh together, love together.

She had to get hold of her thoughts before she made a fool of herself! She rose and put the book on the shelf, keeping her back to him, hoping he was too tired to pay any attention to her. He was thinking aloud. It had nothing to do with her.

"I guess it would be easier, especially if you found a wife who wanted to stay home all day and baby-sit your children," she said coldly. She would hate to be chosen for marriage based on her ability to baby-sit.

"A woman who married me would become the children's mother. I don't think she'd see it as baby-sitting my children."

Cassandra shrugged and crossed the room. "I'll check on the twins and then start dinner. Mrs. Hunter apparently didn't eat here much. There isn't a lot of choice."

"We can order something in. You don't have to cook." Jared rose. He was a big man, Cassandra noticed, and seemed to fill the room just by his presence.

"I don't mind. I like cooking. We might as well use up some of the food, less to waste." She hurried away, away from the thoughts that slipped into her mind and the vague yearnings that arose.

Jared watched her as she left the room. For a moment he toyed with imagining her reaction if he asked her to marry him. She'd been perfect with the twins. He'd feel better knowing someone who knew something about children was partly responsible for helping them grow up.

Of course Helen would locate an experienced nanny. But a hired person could quit and leave. A mother would stay.

Slowly he turned and regarded the now empty chair. He could envision coming home from work each day and finding Cassandra surrounded by children, her hair loose, her glasses on the table and her wide eyes laughing at him as she told him about the children's antics. He'd be able to forget business for a while and share the experiences of his children as they grew.

Frowning, Jared shook his head. Pipe dreams. Cassandra Bowles had made it perfectly clear she was a dedicated businesswoman who, by her last comment, didn't see marriage with a man who had children as something to aspire to. And after his marriage with MaryEllen, he didn't think he wanted a business relationship again. It had worked. They had accomplished what they had set out to do, but next time he wanted more. If there was a next time.

He grabbed his bag and headed for MaryEllen's room. He'd take a quick shower and change into jeans. He wondered if Ashley and Brittany would be even more energetic after a nap. He'd look forward to finding out— and getting to know his little girls better.

Entering the bedroom, Jared stopped as realization struck. There was only one bed, beside the two cribs, in the entire apartment. What were they to do tonight? Granted, MaryEllen's bed was king-size, but he had the distinct feeling that Cassandra wouldn't care if it covered half the apartment—she wouldn't share. For a moment his imagination took over. Cassandra in his bed, her dark glossy hair spread across a pristine white pillow, her face alight with love.

Love? Hardly something to expect from a diehard businesswoman.

The sofa he'd vacated would never do for a bed— curving wooden arms, stiff brocade, as uncomfortable as museum furniture. It looked elegant but did not lend itself to comfort.

He could get a hotel room for the night.

And have Cassandra berate him for deserting his children their first night together? Not likely. He crossed the room, opened his suitcase, took out his jeans and a navy T-shirt and headed for the bathroom.

Maybe he could get her a hotel room.

No, he liked that idea even less. He needed her here in the apartment in case the girls woke during the night. He'd have to come up with something during dinner. Right now a hot shower was as far ahead as he could plan.

By the time he'd finished showering, Jared heard the chatter of little girls. Smiling as he pulled on his jeans, drew his T-shirt over his head, he realized he'd already come to expect some kind of noise around them. They would sure change his place in San Francisco. Change his entire life. He'd have to look for a different apartment, something bigger. Maybe even a house with a yard. Would little girls want a dog? The image of his grandfather's dog came to mind. How would old Ranger have dealt with the twins had he still been alive? Come to that, how would his grandfather?

"Need any help?" he asked a couple of minutes later,

entering the kitchen. Anticipation had already built to see his daughters, to see Cassandra.

The twins turned and ran to him, holding up their arms. He leaned over and scooped both up. "Hi, Ashley, Brittany. Did you have a good nap?"

Ashley smiled and nodded vigorously. "Cassie gib me carrot," she said, holding out the orange sliver.

"Me, too," Brittany said, holding up a matching strip.

"Looks good. Maybe Cassie can gib me one," Jared said, crossing to stand beside her at the sink.

She smiled brightly, her glasses on the counter. For a moment Jared caught his breath. She looked beautiful. Her eyes danced in amusement. Color stained her cheeks, and her hair had slipped from the neat French braid. If he hadn't been holding his daughters, he would have slid a finger through the clasp and released it to let her hair fall around her shoulders.

"I can give you some carrots if you can do the hamburgers. I forgot how impatient hungry kids can be. If we both work at it, we can get the meal on the table faster." Cassandra smiled at the three of them. She hesitated, her smile fading as she took in his casual appearance. She'd never seen him in anything but a business suit before. Somehow the casual navy T-shirt and snug-fitting jeans caused her mouth to grow dry.

He looked heart-stoppingly gorgeous, his hair a bit mussed and his arms full of tiny girls. His fatigue seemed to have vanished. He laughed at something Brittany said. It made him look younger and far, far too attractive. She needed to remember he was her boss.

"Hamburgers?" he asked, raising an eyebrow.

"There was a packet of frozen meat. I thawed it. I've got potatoes cooking in the microwave. I'll finish with this salad, and that will be that. We'll have to have the

burgers without buns. There's no bread in the place."
Cassandra turned to the lettuce she was tearing and tried
to ignore the clamoring of her senses to delve more into
the exploration of this new image of Jared Hunter. She
had work to do, not fantasies to dream about.

"Okay. Want to help me cook hamburgers, girls?"
Jared asked.

"No," Cassandra said, frowning. Didn't the man have
a clue what two-year-olds were capable of? Or not, as
the case may be.

"No?"

"Not around a hot stove. They can set the table."

He set them down and searched for the silverware
drawer. The thought of the twins running with a fork in
each hand sent shivers up his back. "Maybe not. How
about I entertain them and you do the burgers? I don't
mind waiting."

"If you like."

"Cassie play wif me?" Brittany asked, tugging on
Cassandra's jeans.

"I'm busy now, honey, but Daddy will play."

Jared scooped them up and headed for their room,
starting to grow used to being called Daddy by
Cassandra. How soon before his daughters called him
that?

By the time dinner was on the table, Jared had a new
respect for parents everywhere. He had watched the girls
for less than an hour and he was already tired—yet intrigued by these little creatures. Their enthusiasm for everything knew no bounds. They shared easily, including
him in their games, and talked nonstop. He was catching
on to their lingo.

His anger toward MaryEllen simmered. How could
she have denied him the chance to know his daughters?

Had she *ever* planned to tell him? Had he overlooked some clue that would have informed him earlier of their existence?

Dinner proved an adventure. The girls didn't eat much, and half of what they tried to eat went on the floor, the table or their clothes. Taking a clue from Cassandra, however, Jared didn't worry about the mess or correct their behavior.

"They'll eat enough to grow, and the rest can be cleaned up. At least they feed themselves," Cassandra commented at one point, noticing Jared's uncertainty. She'd been around children for years and knew they would eat enough. No sense in making a fuss on their last night in their home. Tomorrow would be fraught with changes. Let them enjoy themselves tonight.

"I dread mealtime on the flight tomorrow," Jared said as Brittany threw lettuce on the table, wrinkling her nose. Maybe it was something she didn't like.

"Discretion being the better part of valor, I suggest we feed them tomorrow on the plane rather than let them do it. It's one thing to let them go in your own kitchen, something else in a public place. Cross your fingers that they don't serve anything in a sauce."

"How many babies did you baby-sit?" he asked. He never would have anticipated how messy sauce would be on a plane. What else was he in ignorance about?

"Lots. Mostly with my foster parents. They cared for a set of twins at one point. But they were older than these two—wild little boys." She smiled. Somehow, looking back, it didn't seem quite so bad. Not that she wanted to get caught up in child care again. She liked her job and was good at it.

"So you have plenty of experience with all ages," he said, studying her thoughtfully.

"Yes." She looked at him warily. His comment from earlier echoed in her mind. If he asked her to marry him to take care of his daughters, she'd throw something!

Jared smiled. "Tell me more about your ideas for GlobalNet. Did you factor into the equation their initial forays into global expansion?"

"Yes, I did, though they are a bit premature. However, I think we can point out the pitfalls and skirt around them for the time being. Once the firm is in a stronger financial position, I have an idea how to ease into what they really want. But it would be a mistake to rush the venture." Without pause she reached out and caught Brittany's glass just before she tipped milk on the table.

For the rest of the meal, they discussed business, interspersed with conversation with the two little girls. Cassandra enjoyed herself and began to relax. It had been a long time since she'd done more than grab a bit to eat at the end of the day, more often than not eating out or having a quick sandwich at her desk while she worked late. She wanted to move ahead as quickly as possible and sometimes stayed hours after the rest of the staff had left.

Jared did not voice his earlier thoughts about finding another wife. Cassandra chided herself for suspecting he'd have such a thought in mind for her. In San Francisco, things would sort themselves out. She'd go back to her own life, and Jared would find someone to take care of his daughters.

"We'll do the dishes," he said when the twins clamored to get down at the end of the meal.

"I don't mind," Cassandra said. Surprised he'd even think to offer, she felt another small kick in her heart. The man was thoughtful when he was not being dictatorial. She wouldn't have expected it. In fact, she was coming to better understand Jared with each passing minute. She'd never quite see him the same way in the office after this trip!

"You fixed dinner. We'll clean up. It was delicious, by the way. Thanks."

"It was hardly gourmet fare. Hamburgers, potatoes and salad."

"Still, it tasted good, and I appreciated not having to do it myself."

"There is that." She smiled at the girls. "Maybe I'll run a bath for them. When you're finished in here, we can pop them in and then get them ready for bed. Annie said they usually go to sleep around eight."

"Did you get all their things packed?"

"All the clothes, some of the toys. The rest will need to be sent. We'll be ready to leave early in the morning."

Which brought up the subject of where everyone would sleep tonight, she thought. Had Jared given any thought to the fact there was only one bed in the place? She watched as he pushed back his chair, stacked the dishes and carried them to the sink. Curious, she said nothing. She had an idea but would wait to see when he broached the subject. In the meantime, she'd make up the bed with fresh linens and run a tub for the twins.

"I'll push two of the chairs over so they can stand on them to be high enough to help," Cassandra said, suiting the words with action. She lifted each child to a chair, admonishing them to be careful, then left him with his daughters. The new family needed time to bond. But she looked over her shoulder as she left, feeling just a little bit left out.

Help was definitely a euphemism, Jared thought a few

minutes later. Ashley loved splashing in the soapy water. Brittany kept putting back the dishes and silverware as fast as Jared could place them in the drainer. At the rate they were going, each of them would be soaked, and it would take until morning to finish the task.

Yet he didn't mind. Watching the joy in their eyes as they *helped* was more than worth the delay. No one had told him how enchanting young children could be. He wished he'd known about them since birth, had seen them take their first steps, heard their first words.

Then maybe he'd have a better chance of understanding them when they talked. He caught most of it, but sometimes they spoke to each other in what seemed to be their own private language. If he listened carefully, he almost caught on.

"Are you all going to stay here all night?" Cassandra asked from the doorway, amusement in her tone.

"Cassie, me help!" Brittany said, turning and almost falling from the chair.

"Watch it, short stuff. Don't fall."

Jared caught her around the middle and set her on the floor.

"Bath time," Cassandra said, laughing softly as she took in the scene. "Though it looks as if you got a head start on me."

He surveyed the wet clothes the twins wore, his damp jeans.

"A new way to cut down on bath time. This is the soapy water phase, all you have to do is rinse them off," he said.

"Right. Come on, girls, you can play for ten minutes, then bedtime."

"Want story," Ashley said as she clambered down from the chair, refusing help from her father.

"Me, too," Brittany said, holding up her arms to Jared. He picked her up, hugged her briefly and set her on her feet. She ran after her sister.

Finishing the dishes in peace, Jared reflected on the day. A series of firsts from the start. He couldn't have managed without Cassandra. He'd have to make sure she knew that.

When they got to San Francisco, he'd ask her out to dinner as a kind of thank-you. Maybe they could try that place near the wharf that featured dancing. They could talk through dinner as they had tonight. Maybe do a little dancing. He'd like to hold her in his arms and move to a slow beat. Feel that softly feminine body press against his as they swayed with the rhythm. Watch for the sparkle in her eyes. Surely she wouldn't wear a suit to dinner. Nor her glasses. Would she arrange her hair in a different style? Or let him unfasten the braid at some point during the evening?

Feeling decidedly un-daddy-like, Jared turned off the light and headed for the bathroom. The sound of splashing and childish laughter grew louder as he approached. Standing in the doorway, he watched as the twins did their best to evade Cassandra's attempts at washing. He liked her dogged determination mixed with laughter and teasing. She was good with them, patient and fun. She was good with *him,* patient and fun. He found his eyes on her more than the children.

Brittany spotted him and grinned. "Man," she said.

Ashley looked up and grinned. He was still amazed at the identical faces that smiled at him.

"Daddy," Cassandra said, looking at him over her shoulder.

"Daddy, daddy, daddy," Ashley chanted. Brittany picked up the chorus.

"I'd offer to help, but you seem to have everything under control," he said.

"Don't you dare leave me alone," Cassandra protested. "Grab a towel and a kid. I'll take the other, and we'll have them ready for bed before they know what hit them."

It took longer than Jared expected, but when the little girls were dressed in matching Lion King nighties, their hair brushed out, smelling sweet and clean, his heart clutched. As he had all day, he tried to absorb as much about them as he could. He had a lot of catching up to do.

"Story," Ashley said.

"Run and get a book, sweetie," Cassandra said, mopping the last of the water from the tile floor. She looked at Jared as he sank to the floor, leaning against the far wall.

Giggling softly, she tossed the towel into the empty tub, sat on the floor and leaned against the tub. "Is this the same man who works through typhoons, letting nothing faze him? You looked wiped out."

"I feel it. Tell me this is because I'm still tired from the Bangkok trip."

Clamping her lower lip between white teeth to hold in her smile, she shook her head. "Might have something to do with it, but it takes a lot of stamina to be a parent."

He rested his head against the wall, closing his eyes until they were open only a slit. She looked flushed from her exertions, warm and feminine. The glasses had stayed in the kitchen. Her hair was almost completely down. He wasn't sure he could resist the temptation to finish letting it fall around her shoulders. When had he become obsessed with her hair?

"We have a shortage of beds," he said slowly.

She looked up and nodded. "But I have a solution. The bed in your wife's room is a king-size one—"

Jared held his breath. She was going to suggest they share? She didn't mind that they scarcely knew each other? It was a big bed, plenty of room for both of them to sleep without bothering the other. If he played his cards right, he'd get to see that shiny dark hair spread on the pillow, see that sexy body in a frilly nightie—

"So I thought we could push it against one wall, and then the girls and I could sleep in it. I'd be on the outside so they wouldn't fall off."

He blinked and stared at her. She and the girls would share the bed? Where did that leave him?

"And I get the cribs?" he asked.

She laughed and shook her head. "Even if you could fit, you'd crash right through to the floor. But I did think you could put the two mattresses together end to end on the floor. That'd be long enough for you. Not the best solution, but it shouldn't be too uncomfortable. Unless you have another idea? I could go to a hotel, I guess."

He knew she would never go for their sharing the bed.

"No, your plan is fine."

Jared rose and held out his hand to assist her up. Cassandra's hand was warm in his, smaller than he'd expected. She stood, her head coming to his chin. He could smell the sweet fragrance of her body, the soft floral scent and the warmth of her skin. It appeared as if she held her breath. Slowly he reached out and flicked the clasp holding her braid.

"Your hair is coming down." Before she could respond, he opened it, clenching the barrette with three fingers while his index finger loosened what remained of her braid.

Her hands tangled with his as she tried to tame her hair.

"I know it's a mess. I thought if you read the story, I could take a quick shower."

"I don't think it's a mess. It looks pretty." Ignoring her hands, he continued to comb through the silky strands until they spread around her shoulders. The bright glare of the bathroom light picked up highlights. Tilting her chin with his finger, he studied the effect. He felt a punch low in his stomach. She was beautiful. Her eyes wide and questioning as they stared into his, her cheeks flushed, her hair a glorious cloud around her face.

"Thank you for helping me with my daughters," Jared said softly. Giving into impulse, he leaned over and kissed her.

For a second he thought she responded. Then she pushed away, stumbling, almost falling into the tub. He caught her, waited until she gained her balance then stepped back.

"I'll see what story they want," Jared said. He waited in case Cassandra had anything to say, but she merely nodded, her look one of startled surprise. He went to find the twins.

"Great," Cassandra mumbled as Jared headed down the short hall, "that had all the finesse of a hippopotamus!" Her boss gave her a brief kiss and she almost fell into a tub! She slapped her hands against her cheeks and she closed her eyes. How gauche could a woman be?

She was sadly out of practice. Not that she'd ever done a lot of dating, and the men she'd gone out with were nothing like Jared. She had not expected a kiss—not from her boss.

Don't make so much of it, she admonished herself. She looked around, stunned. It had merely been a nice thank-you kiss for taking care of his twins. Slowly she let her fingers drift to her lips. Somehow it seemed more than a mere thank-you. She remembered the firm warmth pressed against her, the scent that had filled her, the pounding of her heart. Swallowing hard, she glanced around again as if looking for something. The bathroom was as tidy as they needed for tonight. Tomorrow the cleaning crew would arrive, and later someone from the New York office would take care of closing down MaryEllen Hunter's last home.

Refusing to dwell on the kiss or her stupid reaction, Cassandra headed for the master bedroom. She'd take her shower and be ready for bed when the girls had had their story read.

Jared had pushed the large bed into a corner, urged the girls into it and settled against a stack of pillows to read. The three of them looked up when she walked in.

"I'm just getting my things for my shower," she said self-consciously.

Jared nodded and turned to the story.

In only seconds Cassandra was behind a locked bathroom door, feeling as foolish as ever. What had she expected? That he would say something, try to smooth things over? She was the one who had overreacted.

Conscious of the man in the next room, she slipped out of her clothes and stood under the hot shower. For some reason she felt daring knowing he was so close. She'd never shared a place with a man, never spent the night with one. Never taken a shower with one in her home!

He'd finished the second book when she returned to the bedroom.

"All done?" he asked.

Her hair was damp, hanging in waves down her back.

She'd combed it, but it would have to dry overnight. After donning her sleep shirt, she realized she'd forgotten a robe. Somehow the shirt alone wasn't sufficient covering. She secured a thick bath towel around her, then felt brave enough to face him. Embarrassment seeped in as he looked at her with astonishment. She was wearing a T-shirt, wrapped in a towel, her jeans and shoes clutched to her breast. No wonder—she probably presented a sight.

"Yes. Are you finished with the stories?" She tried to act normal through the extraordinary circumstances.

"We just finished."

She shifted from one foot to the other, "Well, I guess I'll go to bed with the girls. I didn't get much sleep on the plane, and tomorrow will be another long day."

Jared glanced at his watch. It wasn't quite eight. He was so used to being so tired it seemed as if he'd been that way forever. But the dark smudges beneath her eyes attested to the fact she was also exhausted. He could understand why with the events of the last thirty-six hours.

He kissed Ashley and Brittany and scooted them over to make room for Cassandra, then rose, snatched one of the pillows and headed for the door.

Cassandra sidestepped as he drew closer. "Will you wake me in the morning, or do I need to find an alarm clock?"

"I'll get you up at six. Maybe we'll have a chance to get dressed before the angels wake up."

"Right, in your dreams." She smiled shyly and edged toward the bed, dropping her jeans on one of the fancy chairs, setting the shoes beneath it. Jared left, and she took a deep breath. She dragged the towel from around her, then leaned over and began to dry her hair, chatting softly with the twins.

The door opened suddenly. "Sheets! Where would I find bedding for my makeshift bed?" Jared stopped, staring at her. The T-shirt she wore came to the top of her thighs, showing off her shapely, tanned legs, the curves of her body. She swallowed hard at the look in his eye, slowly dropping the towel until it hung in front of her.

"The closet in the hall has linens. I found them when I made up this bed." She had never had a man look at her with such blatant interest. Her heart skipped a beat and settled into a rapid rhythm.

"Right, see you in the morning."

Which may be forever in coming, Cassandra thought a half hour later. The girls had fallen right to sleep. Tired as she was, Cassandra couldn't sleep. Her thoughts spun, keeping her wide awake. Her mind flitted between Jared's kiss and her stupid reaction, then to the echo of his words—maybe he needed a wife—and to her determination to build a career. These twins were adorable, very lovable. How had she gotten so tangled up in only a day?

"Cassandra?" Gently Jared shook her shoulder. She rolled onto her back and her eyes flicked open, then closed. The room was dim. The early morning light did not filter in through the drawn curtains. He had to see from the light in the hall. Cassandra slept on her side, the two twins cuddled up near each other. Even with three of them, the bed looked spacious.

"Hmm?"

He swallowed hard. A mass of wavy dark hair was spread out on the pillow. He could see the petite length

of her beneath the light covers. The urge to slide in beside her was staggering.

"Cassandra, wake up."

Her eyes opened and she stared at him, a soft smile
playing on her lips. Jared resisted the temptation to lean
over and kiss her. Now was not the time nor place to
indulge his yearning. He had a family to get home.

"What time is it?" she whispered, rising on one el-
bow and glancing at the sleeping girls, shaking her head
to clear the last of the sleep.

"Just after six. I've called a cab to pick us up at
seven-thirty. Can you be ready by then?"

"Sure. Did you start coffee?"

"I will." But he made no effort to move, intrigued
by this glimpse of her when she awoke. Was she one of
those people who needed coffee before functioning? Or
was she bright-eyed and eager to get the day started?
Yesterday she'd been cranky. Would she be this morning?

"I'll be dressed in a jiffy," she said, sitting up and
rubbing her eyes with her fingertips.

"Come to the kitchen when you're ready." Reluctantly Jared turned and left the room. He'd start the coffee, see if there was anything perishable they needed to
eat before they left. He'd dressed in comfortable and—
if last night was any indication—necessary jeans. His
bag stood by the door, as did the two for his daughters.
He'd left another for last minute items.

"That smells heavenly," Cassandra said when she entered the kitchen a few minutes later. She had decided
as she dressed to treat the rest of the journey as lightly
as she could. By the end of the day, she'd be home in
her cozy apartment, the trip but a memory.

And if Jared happened to kiss her again—strictly to

thank her for her help—she would not fall apart. She would be prepared!

"You ready to go?"

"Yes, I put my bag beside yours. As soon as we get the girls up and dressed, I can close theirs. Maybe we should plan to eat at the airport, what do you think?" She talked fast, hoping to hide the fact she found him impressive in the early morning. His jeans were faded and old and fit with a comfortable snugness of long wear. His shirt delineated the firm muscles of his chest and shoulders. His skin looked smooth and warm along his jaw. And his eyes—

Cassandra looked away, knowing he'd seen her study him. So much for professional detachment.

"If they can wait that long. Coffee should be ready now."

She fetched two cups when the coffee maker stopped, and filled them. Handing one to Jared, she was careful to avoid touching him. Taking hers, she crossed a comfortable distance away and leaned against the counter, sipping the fragrant brew.

She cleared her throat and asked, "Did you sleep all right last night?"

He shook his head. "Not a bit. The mattresses kept sliding apart. Every time I went to move, I fell through the connection and ended on the floor."

She smiled, taking a sip of coffee to hide it from him. "Sorry about that. At least tonight you'll be home in your own bed. What are you doing about the twins when you get home? Did Helen get cribs for them?"

Jared winced. "Damn, I don't know. I never thought about it." He glanced at the clock.

"Forget it. Don't you dare call her now. It's almost

four o'clock in the morning at home. You can call her from the airport.''

"See how important you are on this venture? Bedtime would have arrived before I thought about cribs.''

"Glad I could help,'' she murmured. In a way, she was. Still a bit miffed he'd made it an order, nevertheless she was glad she could help. And he truly had needed it.

"When we get home, I'd like to take you out to dinner one night,'' Jared said.

Cassandra looked up, her eyes wide. "It's really not necessary.''

"If it were necessary, I probably wouldn't want to do it. In this case, I do.''

"Why?''

"As a thank-you for all this. Consider it a bonus for extraordinary work.''

"When?''

"Friday?''

"What about the girls?''

"I didn't plan to include them.''

"Who will you get to baby-sit?''

Jared had never given that a thought. Wouldn't the nanny Helen hired take care of that? Yesterday afternoon, when he'd talked to Helen, she had not found live-in help. It might take a little while, she'd said. He'd given her until this afternoon.

"I'll find someone,'' he said, suddenly feeling inadequate to the tasks ahead. He knew so little about children and their needs. But he was more than willing to learn, and quickly.

"If you can find a sitter, I'll go,'' Cassandra said slowly, wondering if it were wise. Once they returned home, they'd fall into boss and employee roles. Dating

co-workers was dangerous. Not that dinner would be a
date. He merely wanted to thank her for her help.

Jared was too relieved at her agreement to be annoyed
by her lack of enthusiasm. Or was it caution? Now,
wasn't that an interesting thought. His gaze roamed
across the new T-shirt she wore, then to her snug jeans,
then to her bright pink tennis shoes. She looked young
and carefree and happy even with a dreaded baby-sitting
trek on the plane still ahead. How would she look on
Friday night when he picked her up for dinner and dancing? He could hardly wait.

Jared checked in all the bags except the one shoulder
bag Cassandra insisted they carry on board. The ticket
agent had been most helpful in finding seats together in
a bulkhead row—business class instead of first, but Jared
didn't object. He wanted Cassandra to be close at hand
more than he wanted the comfort of first class.

"What a lovely family you have," one of the passen-
gers commented to Cassandra when she settled the twins
in adjoining chairs in the waiting area.

"Thank you," Cassandra replied, throwing a teasing
glance at Jared.

He met her gaze. What did she think of being tied
with him and his girls? At least she had not made an
announcement that she wasn't the mother and that they
weren't a family. She looked natural. Was there any way
to convince her to stay with him, to become a mother
to his daughters? The idea grew stronger every time it
popped into his mind.

CHAPTER FOUR

THE plane ride went more smoothly than Cassandra anticipated and proved a lot more hectic than Jared had expected. The twins had been fascinated by all the different people, by the movie and the buttons on their seat arms. They had not liked being confined in a small place, however. Once the meal service had been completed, Cassandra took turns walking each twin up and down the aisles until they grew tired. Thankfully, they napped for part of the journey.

Jared tried his best to entertain them when they awoke but was blatantly relieved when the final approach to San Francisco was announced. The flight had seemed longer than the one from Bangkok.

Cassandra smiled as she fastened Brittany's seat belt. Jared was fumbling with Ashley's. "Glad the trip is over?" she asked him.

"Glad we didn't have them on a trip to the Far East. I'm worn out."

"It's hard to stay in one place for long when you're only two," Cassandra murmured, patting Brittany's hand and smiling at the child. Cassandra thought they'd done very well. They were sweet little girls. Already she felt a growing attachment.

Shocked, she pulled away and looked out the window across the aisle. She would not let herself become attached to Jared's daughters. She remembered every time a foster child had left after she'd started to care. How her heart had ached for months, missing them. Even when she'd left of her own volition to go to college, she'd missed Brandon and Sherry and little Tallie. She wondered what had happened to them. Were they happy? Had they also gone to college, found good jobs? A feeling of belonging? Swallowing hard, she shifted her thoughts. She had known Ashley and Brittany but a day, so she couldn't be growing attached. Besides, she could ask Jared about them from time to time. Taking an interest in his children wasn't the same thing as becoming involved.

"I appreciate your help, Cassandra," Jared said as they gathered their belongings to exit from the plane. "This was bad enough with an expert around. I don't think I could have managed alone and kept them so happy."

"You needed someone, that's for sure. But these are good children. You won't have any trouble with them," she said a bit wistfully. They were beautiful children. Jared had a family now, people to whom he belonged and who belonged to him. She had missed that so much growing up. One day, when she was established, she would start her own family.

"Easy for you to say. You'll be home in just a little while. Right now, I'm not sure I can make it through until morning." He lifted Ashley into his arms. Slinging the diaper bag over his shoulder as if he'd been doing it for years, he stepped into the almost vacant aisle and waited for Cassandra and Brittany to precede him.

She flashed him a smile, taking in the charming picture of the large man holding such a tiny, feminine creature. For a moment she felt her heart melt. That way lay danger. Quickly, she walked up the aisle, refusing to let herself feel anything but a professional detachment.

Once she helped Jared get the children home, her task would be finished.

With a feeling of déjà vu, Cassandra spotted a man holding a sign with Jared's name.

"Another limo?" she murmured as they approached the uniformed driver.

"It's cheaper than parking here. And a lot more convenient," Jared answered.

And a lot more luxurious, Cassandra thought a few minutes later when they were speeding toward San Francisco. The girls were buckled safely in their seats, and Cassandra sank back in the soft buttery leather. "I could get used to this," she said appreciatively.

"Saves trouble finding a parking place at home, too," Jared said.

"Where do you live?" Odd she hadn't asked before. Of course, he was her boss. And she had no reason to know.

"Pacific Heights. In a nice old apartment with high ceilings and hardwood floors. Which—" he glanced speculatively at the twins "—I may have to carpet to keep the noise level down. When these two start running around, it'll sound like a herd of cattle."

"Is it large enough for live-in help?" she asked.

"Not really. I'll have to turn my office into a room for the nanny. Put the computer and files in my bedroom, I guess."

Cassandra nodded. There would be a lot of changes in Jared Hunter's life. She studied the two little girls who gazed out the window in wonder. They were so adorable and sweet. She'd dressed them in different colors, to aid in telling them apart. But she already recognized the differences. Their personalities were quite distinct. Did either resemble Jared? Glancing quickly at him, she won-

dered what his full personality was like. She knew he
was patient, witness his dealings with the twins. And he
rose to all challenges without complaint. But was he
truly happy to discover he had twin daughters? Would
he be a loving, involved father? Or delegate their care
to someone else? Would he get married right away just
to obtain a mother for his girls?

For a moment, Cassandra had an overwhelming urge
to insist he take special care of these children. To make
sure he knew how important it was for children to feel
loved and cherished. How devastated they would feel if
he did not. But it wasn't her place.

Jared watched as the expressions chased around
Cassandra's face. What was she thinking? He didn't
know her well, but these last two days had been a crash
course in Cassandra Bowles. She was kind and loving
to two strange children. Snippy and irritated with him
initially. Though he had to admit she'd never shown the
girls a hint of that anger. By dinner yesterday, she'd
seemed resigned to the assignment and had put on a
good face.

A pretty face, actually. He wished she'd take off those
glasses again and loosen her hair. Looking away, he
slowly drew in a deep breath. Thoughts like that led to
the memory of their kiss. And remembering that put him
in mind of other things he'd like to do with Cassandra.

Tomorrow they'd be back at work. Maybe then he
could think of her only as one of his marketing analysts.
An uncomfortable thought came unbidden. What if he
couldn't?

By the time the limousine reached his apartment
building, Jared was growing decidedly nervous. Could
he cope with these girls on his own? He'd called Helen
earlier and, while she'd taken care of the furniture for

the girls, she'd still not located a live-in caretaker. It looked as if he'd be staying home for a couple of days until she found someone.

Cassandra carried Brittany inside the spacious apartment. It was on the first floor, directly over the garages. At least there would be no neighbors beneath them to complain about the twins running around. The hardwood floors gleamed in the afternoon sunshine. The windows were large, stretching almost to the high ceilings, and the curtains were light and airy. She surveyed the furnishings in the huge living room. The word comfortable came to mind. Nothing like the fancy formal furnishing MaryEllen had in the New York apartment. This furniture suited Jared. And was much more suitable for two little girls.

The large stuffed sofa looked inviting. The easy chairs that flanked it had a well-worn look, as if many people had enjoyed sitting in them. There were books in the built-in bookcases, but few knickknacks to tempt a small child.

Slowly she placed Brittany on her feet. The little girl had her thumb in her mouth. She leaned against Cassandra's leg as if afraid to break contact.

"Your room is down there," Jared said, setting Ashley on the floor. She tore down the hall. Brittany watched her.

"Come on, pumpkin, we'll go see your new bedroom. Do you want to?" Cassandra said, reaching for her hand. Curious to see more of his place, Cassandra was glad for the excuse.

The room had been hastily assembled. Two new cribs stood together near the wide window, an old chest of drawers pushed against one wall. There was a disassembled double bed leaning against the opposite wall and a comfortable rocking chair large enough for even Jared to enjoy.

"We'll have to get that bed out before it falls on one of them," Jared said as he followed her into the room. He looked around then gazed at Cassandra. "It doesn't look like their room in New York."

"No, but it won't take much to fix it up. A couple of mobiles and maybe some cutouts of Mickey Mouse or the Sesame Street group on the walls. If you got a toy box or shelves, they could put their toys away. It'll be fine, Jared. I think Helen did a great job in only a day."

"This used to be MaryEllen's room," he said slowly.

Cassandra's eyes widened. She knew they'd had a business marriage but thought it had been the reason for getting married, not that they had not shared a bed. Obviously at one time they had, or the twins wouldn't be here. Not that it was any of her business.

"That'll be nice for them. You can tell them that when they're older."

"If we're still here. I thought I might look for a house or a bigger place. There's a park at the other end of the block but no backyard for them to play in."

"The place I grew up had a huge backyard. We had lots of fun playing there. Sometimes we'd camp out. We felt so brave." She smiled in remembrance. Not everything had been bad in her childhood. She did have nice memories, and thinking about Ashley and Brittany brought some of them to mind.

"Well, I better be going," she said, turning.

"So soon?" Jared asked, all but blocking the door.

Cassandra struggled against a laugh. He sounded positively terrified. "I believe my assignment has ended."

"Stay for supper, at least. We'll order pizza. Then I'll get a cab to take you home."

"All right. But only for pizza. Then I have to get home. Tomorrow is another workday, remember?"

"Thursday. And I suspect if you wanted to take the rest of the week off, the boss wouldn't mind," Jared said. "I'm that grateful for your help."

"I appreciate the thought, but I can't wait to get back to work. I want to get started on the GlobalNet project."

"Of course." Jared's tone cooled considerably. Cassandra looked up, startled at the change. He said nothing further, and she forgot about it when she began to unpack the girls' clothes.

By the time pizza arrived, the twins had explored every inch of the apartment. Cassandra had watched them while Jared moved the disassembled bed to a small room opposite the girls'. He'd set it up later so it would be ready when his hired nanny arrived.

The girls had never had pizza before, and Cassandra hoped the spicy sauce wouldn't upset their stomachs. They massacred a single slice and had a grand time. After a big glass of milk and slightly stale cookies Jared found in the cupboard, they were full and ready for a bath and bed. Despite her intention to leave immediately after eating, Cassandra stayed to help get the twins ready for bed. Bath time was fun, with lots of splashing and giggling. Finally the two were settled in their new cribs.

"Thanks again, Cassandra," Jared said at the door of the apartment when she said goodbye, her bag and briefcase in hand. The cab had arrived, and she had to hurry. But he was reluctant to let her leave.

"All in all, I guess I'm glad I could help," she said honestly. "And you only left them with me once," she teased.

He smiled. She'd had some moments of enjoyment with his daughters. And she was so good with them.

"So I'll see you tomorrow, maybe," she said brightly.

"Call me when you get home."

"Why?"

Jared shrugged, "Just to make sure you got there safely. I'll worry until I know you're home."

Cassandra stared at him. It had been years and years since anyone cared about her, cared if she were safely home at night. Warmth filled her heart. Smiling shyly, she nodded. "Okay, I'll call as soon as I get there. Thanks for dinner."

"If I get a sitter, we're still on for Friday night, right?" he asked, stalling.

"Right. Good night."

Jared reached out and drew her close, his mouth claiming hers in a brief kiss.

Cassandra's senses spun. Before she could react, however, he stood back and brushed his fingertips along her cheek. "Good night."

So much for being prepared if Jared kissed her again, she thought wryly, walking down the single flight of stairs carefully lest she float into the stratosphere. His kisses were amazing and her reactions even more so. But they didn't mean anything. She knew he was grateful for her help with the twins. That was all. A kiss of gratitude.

She tried to think rationally. But a part of her insisted on letting her imagination soar. His hot kisses were only the beginning. Soon Jared would fall madly in love with her, find her fascinating and irresistible. Ask her to marry him and share her life with him. He'd be so crazy about her that he'd do anything to keep her happy. Maybe even make her a partner in Hunter Associates, just like MaryEllen.

Abruptly her daydream ended. What was she thinking of? If he married her like MaryEllen, it would be a business marriage. And she didn't want to get married for years and years, not until she'd made a success of her career.

She suspected Jared planned to get married soon. He would need help with those twins, even with a live-in nanny. And hired help, no matter how competent, was not family. Yet how could any woman be sure marriage to him wouldn't be solely so he could acquire a mother for his daughters? She would hate to be married as a convenience.

Not that any of her suppositions mattered. She had her plans laid out, and they didn't include watching children any time soon. Working had tapped into her creativity, her sense of order. She loved analyzing business, making recommendations for growth. For now, at least, her projects were her babies, and she wanted to see them attain fulfillment.

When she arrived home, Cassandra dialed the number Jared had given her. "Home safe," she reported when he answered.

"Good."

"Are the girls asleep?"

"Yes, haven't heard a peep from them. If Helen can find someone tomorrow, I'll be at the office. If I don't make it in, feel free to call if you have any questions on the GlobalNet project."

"Okay. Will do. Good night."

Businesslike and professional—the phone call was everything Cassandra wanted, so why did she feel so let down?

At work the next day, Cassandra plunged into the GlobalNet project. She kept one eye on Jared's office. She realized by noon that he wasn't going to make an appearance. She wanted to know what Helen had done about a nanny, but wasn't sure it was proper to inquire. Twice she rose to ask and twice sat down. If Jared wanted her to know, he'd have Helen tell her.

By mid-morning on Friday, Cassandra could stand it no longer. She headed for Helen's desk.

"Good morning," Helen said, looking up.

"Hi, Helen. Jared in today?"

"No, I think he'll be back in on Monday. Need anything?"

"Just wondered how he was doing with the twins."

Helen laughed softly. "I think they're running him ragged. But he sounds curiously content with the situation. I found a woman who can move in over the weekend and start watching the girls on Monday, so things should settle into some kind of routine after that."

"Oh, good." There was nothing else to say. Cassandra smiled and turned to leave. The phone rang.

"She's right here." Helen held out the receiver. "It's Jared for you."

"Hello?"

"Hi, Cassandra? Look, I'm sorry about tonight, but I'm going to have to give you a rain check. Helen's found a live-in nurse for the girls, but she won't be here until Sunday, and I don't have anyone to watch them. Can we postpone our date until next week?"

Date? She had thought it a thank-you dinner. She swallowed hard and nodded. Then felt like an idiot. He couldn't see her. "Sure. That's fine. Do you need me to come over tonight to help out?" Where had that come from? She had sworn off watching other people's children. Yet she had missed Ashley and Brittany. A quick visit couldn't hurt.

"No. We're managing. Actually the place is a total

mess, and I'd just as soon not tarnish my image. But
thanks for the offer. Sorry about tonight, I've been looking forward to it.''

"Me, too." She hadn't realized how much until he'd
canceled.

"Put Helen back on, please."

Cassandra handed the phone to the older woman and
quickly returned to her desk. She could work as long as
she wanted today on her current projects. She had no
need to leave early to get ready for a dinner date.
Somehow, the joy in the day vanished. For once the
challenge of her projects didn't consume her.

By the time Cassandra opened the door to her empty
apartment, it was after eight. She'd stopped by a Chinese
place for dinner and wandered around Chinatown for a
little while, window shopping. Feeling at a loose end,
she planned to see if there was anything on television
and maybe go to bed early.

As she changed into comfortable clothes, she remembered waiting for Jared to return to the apartment in New
York. Even though she'd been alone while the girls
napped, a simmering anticipation had filled her. It had
been nice to hear of his day and tell him of hers. Being
married must be like that—to always have someone to
share things with. Which she could do with her friends,
she reminded herself before she could slip into a blue
funk. But it wasn't the same thing.

When the phone rang, she wondered who could be
calling her so late on a Friday night.

"Hello?"

"Cassandra, I need you." Jared's voice came across
the lines calm and dearly familiar.

"For what?" Her heart sped up. Leaning against the
wall, she smiled. It was good to hear his voice.

"Brittany's sick, and I don't know what to do with her."

"What's wrong?" She stood up, instantly worried.

"She's thrown up twice, complains her tummy hurts and won't stop crying. I've tried everything. Nothing seems to work. Any suggestions?"

"I'll be there in ten minutes."

"No, you don't need to come over, just tell me what I should do."

"I'll be there in ten minutes!" Cassandra hung up before he could protest and quickly phoned for a cab. She threw on a jacket and hurried outside impatiently. What could be wrong? Had the baby caught something from the crowd on the airplane? She should have asked if Brittany had a fever. Did Jared have a thermometer? What about fever-reducing medicines? She knew he didn't have any experience with children. She should have made sure the basics were stocked.

Fifteen minutes later she ran up the steps to the first floor and hurried to Jared's door. She knocked impatiently.

Jared opened the door, a crying Brittany in his arms. Ashley hovered nearby, looking upset.

"Oh, baby, are you sick?" Cassandra reached for the little girl, who lunged for her. Scooping her close, she hugged her, resting her cheek against the baby's forehead. "No fever, just warm from crying, I think." Relief flooded her. She had imagined all sorts of things on the cab ride over.

"God, I'm glad to see you, but I didn't want to interrupt your evening."

"No problem, my date canceled," she said sassily. "Come on, babykins, tell Cassie what's wrong."

Brittany snuggled closer and cried softly, her tears wetting Cassandra's cheek. "Tummy hurts," she said.

Cassandra rubbed her back and smiled brightly at Ashley. "Hi, honey, how are you feeling?"

"Fine. Bitnee sad."

"Yes, I see that. But she'll be fine soon." Stepping into the kitchen, Cassandra looked at the chaos. There were plates and glasses stacked in the sink. Pans were on the stove and the trash was overflowing. She looked at Jared.

"Pretty bad, huh?" he said, looking at everything as if for the first time. "It's hard to get things done with two babies underfoot all day."

"And when they nap?"

"That's the only time I have for work. I do have a business to run, remember?" he said testily.

"Excuses, excuses," Cassandra teased. Opening one cupboard after another, she searched for soup.

"What are you looking for?" Jared asked.

"Chicken noodle soup. You do have some, don't you?"

"Not that I know of. But canned goods are over here." He opened a cupboard and began reading labels. Surprised, he lifted down a can. "I do have some."

"Probably courtesy of Helen. Heat it up, and we'll see if that makes this baby feel better."

Jared ran his fingertips over Brittany's cheeks, brushing her hair from her flushed face. "She'll be okay?"

"I think so. What did she have to eat today?"

Jared poured the soup in a saucepan, followed the directions on the can and turned on the burner. "Just the same food she's been eating for two days. Except for the cotton candy."

"Cotton candy?"

"We went to Pier 39 today, to ride the merry-go-round. And I bought them some cotton candy."

Cassandra looked at Ashley. "Does your tummy hurt, honey?"

She shook her head.

"Do you think it was the candy?" Jared asked. "Ashley didn't like it, said it was too sugary."

"Too sweet for her, huh? Too much sugar will make them hyper and could upset their stomachs."

Jared rubbed his eyes. "I don't know how to be a father."

"Don't be silly, you're doing a great job. That was nice to spend the day at the pier, and I bet they loved the merry-go-round. But at this age, I wouldn't give them much beyond the bland foods they're used to. I was worried the other night about the pizza. They didn't eat too much, so it didn't upset their stomachs."

"I remember going to a fair once and getting cotton candy. It was so good."

"And you were probably older," Cassandra said, gently rocking. Brittany had stopped crying and snuggled close.

"I guess I was about nine."

"A tough little boy who could handle anything, even cotton candy."

Jared smiled slowly. "I thought so in those days."

Cassandra's heart pounded. Heat slowly spread through her. Jared was devastating when he smiled. Her mind went blank. All she could do was feel the shimmering sensations that rushed through her as she stared at the man. She looked away quickly, afraid she'd melt into a puddle with Brittany in her arms if she didn't gain some perspective. So he was handsome as sin. She had worked with handsome men.

She could handle this.

"Um, have you considered that if you don't tidy up a bit, your new nanny will take one look at this place and flee for her life?" Cassandra said, trying to get her emotions under control.

"Taken care of. Tomorrow my cleaning service is scheduled. I'm not crazy. The last thing I want to do is scare the woman away. Who would have thought it would be so tough to find a live-in nanny for two little girls? Helen had a terrible time."

"I hope it works out. Is the soup warm yet?"

After Brittany had a few sips of soup, she seemed improved. Ashley stayed close to her sister. Only when Brittany laughed at something Cassandra said did she relax.

"I want Mommy," Ashley said to Jared, tugging on his sleeve.

He went completely still, gazing at his daughter.

"Your mommy's dead, honey. She's gone to live in heaven," Cassandra said gently as the silence stretched out.

"Should you tell them that?" Jared asked sharply. He looked angry. "They're just babies. When they asked earlier, I told them she had gone away."

"They are babies and probably will ask you a dozen times or more for their mommy. If you say she's gone away, it implies she'll be back. When she doesn't return, they'll question your credibility. They need the truth, no matter how difficult it is. And the truth is their mommy is dead and is never coming back for them. But they have their daddy, and he will take care of them. They need reassurance, Jared. Give them that, but don't lie to them."

"It seems so harsh."

"It is. But so is life sometimes. I think it's terrible they lost their mother so young. But they're lucky in that they have a father who will love them and take care of them."

"So they don't go to foster care or have to live with a cantankerous old grandfather," he murmured, caressing Ashley's head.

"Who did that?" Brittany struggled to get down. Cassandra set her on her feet and watched as she and Ashley rushed off to their room, sounding like that herd of cattle Jared had predicted.

"Me. My parents died when I was ten. I went to live with my grandfather. He wasn't pleased to have to raise me. He'd been a widower for years and had his life just the way he wanted. Raising a ten-year-old boy wasn't his idea of a peaceful retirement, but he was all I had. He had no choice."

"I'm sure he loved you."

Jared shrugged. "Maybe, but it wasn't a normal family life that most kids enjoy. I'd like for my girls to have a father *and* a mother."

Cassandra looked away. She would be happy for him if he found some nice woman who would marry him and raise his children. The pang in her heart had nothing to do with disappointment or an unidentified yearning.

"So we are both orphans," she said as she rinsed the soup bowl. The rest of the soup she'd put in the refrigerator in case they needed it later.

"Yes. Which is something I don't want for my children." Jared leaned against the counter, watching as she stacked dishes in the sink, running water to let them soak.

"Better take care of yourself, then. You should live to be an old man. Is your grandfather still living?"

"Sure is. Eighty-three and going strong."

"What does he think about the girls?"

Jared shook his head. "He doesn't know about them yet. I thought I'd drive up next weekend and introduce them. I imagine it'll come as quite a shock. It was for me. He lives in Sonora. Want to come with us?"

Yes, Cassandra wanted to shout. She would love to spend a day with Jared and the twins next weekend. But caution warily took hold. "I don't think so, but thank you for asking me."

"Well, I can't blame you. Baby-sitting on your day off probably doesn't hold much appeal."

"It isn't that. I'd love to spend the day with you and the girls. But it's a family outing. I'd be an outsider." She'd had enough of that experience to last her a lifetime.

"No more than I feel around the twins. Come with us. Have you ever been to Sonora?"

She shook her head.

"You'll love it. It's an old gold mining town. Columbia is just a few minutes away. It's been restored to look just as it did during the gold rush. We could wander around and soak up a bit of history, education for the children, you know."

Cassandra laughed. "Right, like a two-year-old is going to learn a lot of California history."

"You never know what they'll pick up. We'll have lunch and visit with Grandpa. He'll probably nap when the girls do. But I'd bet he'll watch them in the evening, and we could have that dinner together—just the two of us."

"That would mean going for the weekend," she said slowly. The picture he painted tantalized. She'd love to see some of the country. And spend time with Jared.

Childish laughter sounded in the distance, but Cassandra scarcely noticed. She was mesmerized by the intensity of Jared's dark eyes, by the pull of attraction that threatened to spring out of control. And by the enticing image of a weekend in the gold country.

"Is there a problem? Do you have something else planned?" His voice was low and deep. Its attraction pulled, as did the look in his eyes. Swallowing, Cassandra tried to discover a reason she should say no, but found none. It couldn't hurt to spend a couple of days with the Hunters. And she would get to see a part of the state she had not visited. It was always good to expand one's knowledge about history.

"I guess there's not a problem. What time do you want to leave?" she asked.

He smiled again. Maybe she should warn him about doing that. If he wanted her to keep any sense at all, he had to stop. But in the meantime, she'd enjoy the shivers that danced up her back.

"We'll leave early. It takes about four hours."

"Add another half hour at least, to allow for extra stops."

"What extra stops?"

"Obviously you've never traveled with kids. Trust me on this, you'll have to stop several times."

"You're the expert. We'll leave at seven-thirty."

Cassandra looked around the kitchen. "Want help in here before I go?"

Jared stepped closer. "No. I told you the cleaning service is coming in the morning. They can handle it. Do you have to leave? Stay until after the girls are in bed. We didn't get dinner, but maybe we could spend a little time together. Unless you had other plans?"

"No, no other plans. And it's after nine. They should be in bed."

Cassandra considered the fire she was playing with. It was dangerous, but she had no inclination to leave. She liked being with Jared. And he could teach her so much about business. Maybe they could work a trade—child-care suggestions in exchange for coaching in business situations.

Putting the girls to bed was fun. Once they had their nighties on, all of them snuggled together on Jared's sofa to read Dr. Seuss's *Green Eggs and Ham*. Cassandra had read that book so many times she could recite sections without looking. Ashley and Brittany thought it wonderful. And she suspected Jared did, as well, from his look of amazement.

"You feel all better, Brittany?" she asked as she tucked the toddler in her crib.

"Bitnee better. Where's Mommy?"

"Mommy is in heaven. She misses you like you miss her. But your daddy's here, and he'll take care of you forever and ever."

Kissing the little girl on her cheek, Cassandra smelled the baby fresh skin with its hint of talc. Why did babies smell so good? They were precious enough without that added bonus.

She went to kiss Ashley while Jared bid Brittany good-night. Then the two adults crept into the living room.

"They should be asleep in five minutes, if they stick to their routine," Jared said, stretching. He rolled his shoulders and looked at Cassandra.

"Thanks for staying, Cassie."

She raised her eyebrows at the diminutive.

"Do you mind?" he asked.

"Calling me Cassie?"

"The girls do it. They talk about you all the time. I guess I think of you now more as Cassie than Cassandra."

"It's fine." Feeling flustered, Cassandra moved to look out the large window. The view of the apartment building across the street was not particularly inspiring, but it did look nice with lights shining from the windows.

"If you open the window and look to your right, you can catch a glimpse of the bay," he said, moving to stand right behind her. As he reached to unfasten the window, Jared pinned her between his hard body and the windowsill.

Cassandra resisted temptation to press herself against him. She watched as his long fingers unlatched the window and raised it. She stuck her head out and looked. In the distance she caught a glimpse of the sparkling lights on the Bay Bridge, their reflection dancing on the dark water.

"So this is a bay view apartment," she murmured as she ducked her head inside and stood up. She was trapped by Jared.

"So they said when we rented. Does your apartment have such a view?" His voice was low, seductive. He didn't move, just waited patiently as if to see what she would do.

Heart pounding, Cassandra vainly attempted to ignore the excitement that exploded. He was inches away. She felt his warmth encircle her just as his arms encircled her.

Mesmerized, she froze as his head slowly descended. Giving herself up to the pleasure she knew he promised, she closed her eyes and met his kiss.

Had she waited all her life for such a kiss? His lips were warm and firm and oh-so-sexy as they moved against hers. He banded her to his hard length, and she reveled in the sensations that raged. Her arms fought for freedom, then encircled his shoulders, her fingertips tracing the edge of his hair, plunging in to feel the thickness, the heat. To hold on when her knees grew weak and her legs threatened to give way.

Breathing became difficult, but she didn't care. Her heart pounded so hard she could feel it against her chest. She never wanted to move. It was heaven on earth to be kissed by Jared Hunter.

"Daddy!" A splash of ice water could not have ended the kiss any faster.

Jared turned and hurried into the bedroom. Cassandra took a deep breath and leaned against the windowsill. The coolness of the night began to counter the heat of his kiss, and in a moment she regained a modicum of common sense. Once she felt under control, she closed the window. Straightening her glasses, she wondered if she should leave.

An involvement with Jared was foolish. He would want more from her than she could give. He'd almost admitted he planned to acquire a mother for his daughters. Was he pretending something else to lure her into accepting an offer?

It was hard to be practical sometimes. How could a few kisses hurt? He knew she was intent on building a career. As long as she made herself clear, he would understand. She suspected he would soon make a concerted effort to find a wife. But in the meantime, they could spend a little time together.

And she enjoyed being with Ashley and Brittany.

Smiling, she remembered their funny rendition of the merry-go-round. They had been so enchanted with it.

"Sorry about that. Ashley wanted a glass of water." Jared returned to the living room but stayed near the door.

"A classic stalling technique. Effective, too. Now she'll be up sometime in the night needing the bathroom."

He smiled and nodded. "Same as last night. But I don't mind."

Taking a deep breath, Cassandra pushed away from the window and went to sit on the sofa, refusing to let her disappointment show. There was no reason for him to resume kissing her. Though from the way he looked at her mouth, she knew he was considering it.

CHAPTER FIVE

JARED sat on the sofa beside her, careful to leave an appropriate and safe distance between them. Stretching his long legs out in front of him, he leaned his head against the cushions. "I'm tired. Those two can run a person ragged."

Cassandra was touched by the vulnerability she spotted. At the office he seemed so hard, so distant. He was not known to tolerate incompetence or sloppy work. She was fascinated by this private glimpse of him at home. The evidence of how different his life was now showed in the toys strewn about and the dirty dishes in the kitchen. Yet he had not lost his temper with his children. And he had made the day memorable by taking them to a merry-go-round. Her heart melted a little at the attempts this man was making to cope with instant fatherhood.

"They have so much energy. Yet think how exciting everything is for them at that age. So much to discover," she said.

"And so much danger. I thought I'd lost Brittany at one point today at the pier. For a few awful moments I feared she'd fallen into the water or that someone had kidnapped her. And taking two little girls to the rest room isn't as easy as you might think."

Cassandra laughed softly. "Jared, I really like your daughters, but do you think we could not talk about them for a while?"

He turned his head slightly to look at her. "Antichildren. I almost forgot."

"Sort of, I guess."

"Too bad. You're so good with them."

"People can be good at things they don't like."

"Deliver me from being a doting father who bores everyone with tales of his brilliant children," he murmured.

"It's not that, Jared. They're adorable. I really like them. But—"

"But you have a career and no time for kids."

"I guess." Put that way, it sounded so cold. Cassandra frowned. It wasn't that she didn't want children at some point, just not now.

"If the twins are off limits, so is business," Jared countered.

Cassandra stared at him. She'd wanted to pick his brain, explore different avenues of the projects she was working on. Obviously he'd seen through her.

"Fine. You pick a topic."

"I pick you," Jared said, smiling wickedly.

"Me? There's nothing remotely interesting about me. Besides, you already know everything about me."

"What I know is that you were born in L.A. and now live here. Somewhere along the way you went to college. As I recall from the interview, you had a list of impressive achievements."

Basking in the glow of his unexpected compliment, Cassandra relaxed. "I love chocolate ice cream and like to read more than watch television. I like nice clothes but am secretly more comfortable in jeans. Is that what you want to know?"

"It's a start. What kind of books do you like to read? I like mysteries, myself."

Time seemed to fly as the conversation shifted from books they liked to movies they had and had not seen. Jared spoke of the travel he'd done for the company, and Cassandra confessed her longing to visit exotic locales.

When Jared rose to check on the girls, Cassandra almost went with him. She knew she was being foolish to keep a distance from the twins. Every child benefited from love, no matter who gave it. But she was afraid she'd get caught up in feeling needed and wanted to the detriment of her professional goals. It would be so easy for a woman who had never had a family to yearn for one. To forget for a moment her true goals and give in to the fantasy of being part of a loving family.

"Asleep?" she asked when he returned.

"Fast asleep. Thanks for your help with Brittany. I didn't know what to do."

"You need to get a pediatrician. If she had been really sick, you would have had to go to the hospital and take whoever was on call."

"There's more to this parenting that I expected."

"And you've only just started," she said with a smile. "But you're doing great, Jared. Don't worry about it."

"I like feeling in control, and this evening I felt anything but. I think women are better at this than men. If I had a wife, she'd have known what to do."

Cassandra's heart fell. "Being a woman doesn't automatically mean she comes with an instruction booklet on how to raise children. Many men successfully raise children. And there are a lot of career women who haven't a clue."

"Like Helen. I called her before you, and she didn't have a single idea except to call you."

Feeling a bit deflated at being second choice,

Cassandra checked her watch. "It's late. I should be going."

"I'll call a cab. Thanks for staying. Talking with toddlers for two days, I was starved for adult conversation."

Cassandra didn't think he looked starved for anything. She watched him dial the taxi service. His snug jeans looked worn and comfortable. He'd mentioned he also liked casual clothes more than business attire. Somehow he looked even sexier in his faded jeans than his Armani suits. The way his broad shoulders filled his shirt sparked her memory of how those shoulders felt beneath her questing fingertips. She rose abruptly and wandered around the room, trying to escape her thoughts.

Would he kiss her again before she left? Just thinking about the possibility had her tingling.

"It'll be here in just a few minutes. I didn't realize how late it was. Time went fast." Jared went to the window to watch for the cab.

"I had fun. I'm glad Brittany's okay. Upset tummies usually have a fast recovery. If she'd been truly ill, I think Ashley would have been feeling bad, too."

"I wish I could walk you downstairs or even see you home," Jared said, leaning against the wall beside the window. He could see the street and watch her at the same time.

"I'll be fine."

"Call me when you get there."

That unexpected warmth again. She nodded.

"He's here." Jared crossed to her and rested his hands on her shoulders. "I'll see you at the office next week. Then on Saturday we'll go to Sonora. Wear jeans, but bring a dress for dinner."

"Okay." She was having trouble breathing. Every

breath filled her with his special scent, a hint of musk and something else that was uniquely Jared.

He stared into her eyes for a long moment. Cassandra held her breath, too uncertain to initiate a kiss yet yearning for one with all her heart. Surely he'd kiss her goodnight. He'd kissed her earlier. Another thank-you kiss. A goodbye kiss would be different, wouldn't it?

"You'd better go," Jared said, squeezing her shoulders gently and releasing her.

"Bye." She almost ran from the apartment. Had he suspected how much she wanted a kiss? She'd die of embarrassment if he had. But she had played it cool. Settling in the back of the cab, she glanced up at the lighted windows. He waved. She waved back and wished more than ever that he'd kissed her again.

On Monday Cassandra beat Jared to work by a solid ten minutes. At her desk when he arrived, she let herself enjoy looking at him, her gaze following him when he strode off the elevator. Already focused on the business at hand, he never glanced her way. Disappointed, she plunged into work, trying to convince herself it was what she wanted. This was business. No time for personal agendas. But a quick wave or smile wouldn't have hurt.

Still, she had the weekend to look forward to. Two days with the twins and their sexy daddy.

Sexy? She stared blankly at the paper but saw only Jared's dark hair, tousled. Saw his laughter when listening to Ashley explain something, the intensity of his eyes just before she closed hers when he kissed her. He was sexy—and off-limits. She had work to do! Heat stole into her cheeks, and she ruthlessly brushed aside her thoughts before they distracted her so she couldn't do her job.

She didn't see Jared the rest of the day. Curious as to how he liked the new nanny, she wished he'd at least stopped by her desk long enough to tell her about the woman.

The first thing on the day's agenda on Tuesday was the regular staff meeting for project managers. Cassandra took her usual seat at the far end of the table from Jared. He joined the gathering at precisely nine and instantly began requesting information to bring him up to speed on various projects. When it was Cassandra's turn, she spoke clearly and concisely. His gaze never wavered from her face while she spoke, but there was nothing in his expression to suggest he'd kissed her several times and had invited her to spend the weekend with him and his family in four days.

His treatment was professional and courteous, as with all his staff. The meeting went on a long time, since Jared had been away from the office for over a month. Cassandra took a late lunch when the meeting ended. The wind was brisk in the city streets, refreshing and invigorating. Cassandra loved to wander around at lunchtime when the weather permitted. San Francisco continued to charm her. Taking her deli sandwich to Union Square, she found a sheltered bench and basked in the sunshine, the cool air whipping strands from her neat French braid.

She and her team were making good strides on the GlobalNet project. She was in the last stages of two other projects and already thinking ahead to a new idea for an old client. Her career seemed firmly established. In time she might even think of opening her own firm or going into partnership with someone.

Jared sprang to mind.

Giving in to the inevitable, she let herself dream about

becoming a partner with him. They could travel together. Expand the company until theirs was one of the premier firms in international consulting in the Pacific Rim. She liked analyzing business directions and devising plans. How much more exciting would her job be as her expertise grew?

But her thoughts didn't stay on business opportunities. They veered to Jared himself. Remembering when she'd watched him pick up a daughter and toss her in the air, taking delight in her joy. Remembering him tired and quiet on the sofa, discussing music that appealed to him in different moods. She remembered Jared vulnerable and uncertain about how to provide the best for his babies. The strongest memories were of Jared's kisses.

Cassandra sat up abruptly. Crushing the paper that had wrapped her sandwich, she rose, ready to return to work. She'd wasted enough time in foolish daydreams.

When Cassandra arrived at work on Thursday, the place was humming. A major client was expected at ten. The presentation the senior management team had prepared, if sold, would bring in a huge influx of cash and push the reputation of Hunter Associates even higher. While Cassandra had not been involved in the project, she felt the same air of anticipation the team members did. She wanted the presentation to go well. She took pride in her firm.

Shortly before ten, Helen hurried to her desk, a worried frown on her face.

"Cassandra, can I speak to you privately?" Helen asked, her gaze darting nervously at the nearby desks.

"Of course." Cassandra rose and followed Helen to Jared's office. Helen closed the door behind them.

"We've got an emergency on our hands. The nanny I hired for Jared quit without notice this morning. I'm trying to get someone, but so far no luck—at least I can't get anyone to watch the girls immediately. And the presentation to TelStar is due to begin in less than a half hour. Jared has to be here. I don't know what else to do. Would you go watch the girls?''

"Me?" Cassandra asked. Not again!

"I know it isn't your regular job, but this is an emergency. If I could tell Jared you're coming, it would go a long way to relieving his mind. The girls know you, and you know how to handle them. I wouldn't ask if it weren't so important. Please?''

"Did Jared ask you to get me?" Cassandra asked, growing cold at the thought of her hard work being ignored so she could function as a convenient nanny.

"No. He thinks I'm still trying the different agencies. If you refuse, I might have to go myself, and I don't know anything about children. Plus I was to provide the coffee for the group and be ready to make photocopies if needed, or take a quick fax.'' Helen wrung her hands, obviously upset. "Of all the days for this to happen. Why the woman couldn't have waited the week out I don't know. Please, Cassandra, it's just for today. Tomorrow Jared can stay home with them until I can find another baby-sitter. But not today. This meeting is too important.''

"Let me think," Cassandra said, trying to remember all she'd planned to do that day. "I was analyzing some of the Hong Kong information from GlobalNet.''

"Use Jared's computer at home—it's linked up to the one here. He uses it all the time. If you can work from there, all the better. How about it?'' Helen looked at the clock. It was almost nine forty-five.

"Okay. I'll get my papers and leave immediately.''

"Let me call Jared first." Helen punched in his phone number.

"Jared? No, I didn't find anyone yet, but Cassandra said she'd watch them... Okay, I'll tell her." Helen hung up and grinned.

"Thank you, Cassandra. Jared said you saved his life and that of the firm and he'll be forever in your debt. He's bringing the girls here. You can meet them downstairs. There's no time for him to wait for you to get there before leaving for the office. Not if he wants to be on time for the meeting."

"That'll give me a chance to get my stuff together."

Feeling torn, Cassandra returned to her desk. She was glad to help—she wanted to be viewed as a team player. But somehow she didn't see a role as chief baby-sitter doing much to advance her career. Still, it was nice to have the owner of the firm feel in her debt.

In the lobby, Cassandra waited. She had all the materials she needed to finish her analysis of the Hong Kong market in her briefcase. As long as she could use Jared's home computer, she'd be fine. Of course she'd only be able to work when the girls napped, but at least she'd have a few hours. And maybe she could bribe them with "Sesame Street" or something else on television to keep them occupied.

Jared hustled through the tall glass doors, a child's hand in each of his. The little girls had to run to keep up with his long stride. He looked harried and rushed—and downright wonderful. Cassandra felt her heart rate increase.

"Cassie, you're a wonder." He leaned over and kissed her lightly. Stooping to eye level with the twins, he looked at them. "You two be good for Cassie. Mind her and don't get into trouble. Okay?"

Both girls nodded solemnly.

"'Kay, Daddy," Ashley said.

"Me, too," Brittany said, then gave Cassandra a sunny smile.

He rose and handed them over to Cassandra. "I don't know how late I'll be. I had planned to take the clients to dinner, but if I can get out of it, I will."

"Don't worry about it, Jared. Do what you need to get the contract. I'm going to use your computer and can keep working tonight if you're late. I'd probably get more done once they're in bed. Good luck."

His eyes gazed into hers for a long moment. "Thanks, Cassie, I owe you." He brushed his lips against hers again and strode to the elevator.

She watched him wistfully, wishing she was going back to the office with him, wishing she were participating in the presentation.

"Cassie play wif me?" Ashley asked, smiling.

"Yes, Cassie will play with both of you. But first we have to go to my house so I can change my clothes. Then we'll go to the park, have lunch and take a long nap. Won't that be fun?"

When the girls napped, Cassandra took her briefcase and headed for the door to Jared's bedroom. Conscious of the rumpled king-size bed that dominated the room, she gazed around, looking for the computer. It was set up on a small table against the opposite wall. She stepped inside and took a breath. The room smelled like Jared. Instantly her senses came alive. Gazing at the bed, she saw the left pillow still bore the indentation from his head. So he slept on that side. Did he every night? He was a big man, probably liked the space the huge bed provided.

His closet door was slightly ajar, displaying a row of

suits and shirts. She closed it lest she found herself distracted. It was bad enough to have his bed just a few feet behind her. There was a bathroom adjacent to the bedroom. Spotting his shaving paraphernalia, she walked to the door and studied the room. He hung up his towels and didn't leave his clothes lying around, she observed. But the cans and jars sitting on the counter looked foreign to her eyes. She'd never shared a bathroom with a man. What would it be like? Would he mind if she perched on the edge of the tub and watched him shave? Did he do it right after a shower, or did he partially dress first?

Stepping back, Cassandra shook her head. She had a few precious hours to work while the babies slept. There was no time to daydream the minutes away.

It was after ten when Cassandra heard the key in the lock. Jared came into the living room and stopped when he saw her. Slowly he smiled.

"How did it go?" she asked, rising from the sofa. She'd just finished her analyses a few moments ago and was glad to be in the living room rather than in his bedroom. Her glasses were on the table, and she'd let down her braid, running her fingers through her hair while she worked on the complex numbers. She should have brushed her hair. Too late now.

"They signed at four this afternoon. We went to dinner at the Blue Rose. I just dropped them at their hotel."

"Congratulations! I knew you could do it. I've heard about the plan from Bob Farrel. It sounded ambitious but made perfect sense. With a little bit of luck, it should implement flawlessly." She grinned as happily as if it had been her project.

"I'm counting on it." He shrugged out of his jacket

and tossed it on the back of the sofa. "How were the girls?"

"Angels. They are very well behaved."

He rubbed his eyes with his fingertips, then looked at her, slowly shaking his head. "Not with Anthea Good. She was the nanny Helen hired."

"What happened?" Cassandra wished she felt comfortable enough to touch him, to offer a bit of comfort to ease his frustration.

"She'd been watching a young teenage girl for a family in Hillsdale who just got transferred to Belgium. Not wanting to move to Europe, she gave notice. But I suspect from what she said that the girl was a paragon of perfection. Ashley and Brittany seemed to be much more rambunctious. Into everything, according to Anthea."

"But why give notice in the middle of the week? Didn't she realize how that could impact on you?"

"I don't think she cared. This morning while she was dressing, the girls got into her makeup in the bathroom and made a huge mess—of themselves. And spilled or dumped all her bottles and creams. They mixed powder in with toothpaste for a nice effect."

Cassandra burst into laughter. "I bet they thought they were beautiful. Now I know what they meant when they said they were pretty this morning. So Anthea didn't appreciate that, huh?"

"I'm just as glad she's gone. She was too old for them, I think. Always wanted them to sit quietly. I have yet to see them sit quietly."

"Except when being read to," Cassandra said, a smile still lighting her face.

Jared stared at her, his attention drawn from his daughters to the woman before him. She continued to fascinate him. He'd tried to keep his interest to a professional level. Even managed on Tuesday to treat her like every other employee. But seeing that dark hair swirling around her shoulders made his fingers itch to touch it. Her eyes sparkled at him, no longer hidden behind the guardian glasses. She had looked as happy with the success of the TelStar proposal as he had felt.

He wished she had been at the meeting, had attended the celebration dinner. It would have been nice to have someone who would be pleased for his success beyond what it added to the company's bottom line. To be genuinely happy for him.

"I appreciate your filling the gap so quickly. This afternoon Helen found a young woman who will able to watch them during the day. She'll continue to look for live-in help. It seems to be a bigger problem than I thought to hire someone."

"Time for you to get that wife you keep talking about," Cassandra said lightly.

Jared nodded, watching as she gathered her things. His one foray into marriage had not been typical. For all the years he and MaryEllen had been married, they had spent remarkably little time together. And when they had, more often than not their conversation had focused solely on business. He felt he knew more about Cassandra after a week than he'd known about MaryEllen in all the years they'd been together.

Cassandra would never have hidden the fact that he'd become a father.

But she was consumed by business, just like MaryEllen.

Jared looked up the phone number of the taxi service. "I ought to set this number in speed dial," he said as he punched the keys.

He saw her hesitate, then raise her head to look at

him, wary caution in her gaze. "I don't plan to make this a habit."

"I sure hope we don't. You're too talented to spend all your time with children."

Grimly he watched her bloom beneath his casually spoken words. She was great with his children. It wasn't only the experience she'd garnered while growing up, it was her innate warmth and genuine interest. She was talented in business savvy, but she was gifted in dealing with children.

Jared watched from the window when Cassandra got into the cab. This made the third time. Wasn't there some saying about it being a lucky charm? He was getting used to this. Though he wished he could take her home, see her apartment, learn a little more about her from seeing what she found important in her life.

Knowing almost to the minute how long it would take before she phoned, he checked on the girls and headed for his bedroom. He noticed the unmade bed. He should have at least pulled the covers up that morning. What had Cassie thought when she saw it? He looked at the computer. The desk was immaculate. She'd stacked his papers in one corner, probably to give herself space to spread out her own. Loosening his tie, he crossed to the chair and touched it lightly, trying to envision her working here. He could imagine her serious expression as she became caught up in the work. He'd noticed it once or twice over the years she'd worked for him.

Could he detect a faint hint of roses? Closing his eyes, he remembered their trip to New York. It seemed like a lifetime ago instead of only days.

By the time the requested call came, he had climbed into bed, conscious all at once of how big it was, and how lonely.

"I'm home safe."

He smiled in the dark. He liked the sound of her voice. Soft and lilting.

"Good. I forgot to ask if you were able to get any work done today."

"Yes, I managed a good two hours while they napped. Then when they went to bed, I finished up. Actually, with no one around to interrupt, I got a lot done. Nothing along the line of getting that TelStar contract signed, however. You must feel so proud about that."

"I'm pleased, I have to admit. We worked long and hard, and I'm sure our projections are going to be right on the money."

"I better go. You should get to bed."

"I'm already in bed."

There was a long pause. Jared wished he could see her expression.

"You are?" she said at last.

"Six a.m. comes mighty early. And that seems to be the time Ashley loves to run and jump in my bed."

"With Brittany right behind, I imagine."

Jared chuckled. "They surprised me to death that first morning. It was as awkward as hell, too. I used to sleep nude. I wasn't sure if I was ever getting out of bed that day."

Cassandra's soft laughter floated across the telephone line. Jared tightened his grip on the receiver. He wished she'd stayed a bit longer tonight. He enjoyed talking with her. And he suspected he'd just shocked her.

"So what did you do?" she asked.

"Tricked them into running to their room to get a book. Then I dashed from the bed, grabbed some jeans and barely made it to the bathroom before they came back. They're as quick as greased lightning, you know."

"I know. So now you chastely wear pajamas?"

"Just the bottoms. I get too hot in bed to wear a top. They're fascinated by my chest hair."

The silence on the other end was telling. Jared smiled again. "Cassie? What are you thinking?"

It came in a rush. "Actually I'm thinking this is a totally inappropriate conversation to be having with my boss and that I had better stop before I melt into a puddle, and that I can imagine the twins' fascination. I'd probably share it. Oh, Lord! I have to go."

She cut the connection.

Jared held the phone until the dial tone started. Interesting reaction. She couldn't be as immune as he'd suspected. He hung up gently, then cradled his head in his stacked hands, gazing up in the dark. Interesting woman, Cassie Bowles.

She hadn't said that! Please, someone tell her she hadn't admitted to sharing the twins' fascination with Jared's chest hair. Heat flooded her cheeks. She would never be able to face him. Tomorrow she'd fax in her resignation, cancel the trip this weekend and screen her calls forever!

She dragged herself to the bedroom and changed into her light cotton nightie. As she washed her face, she gazed in the mirror, not surprised to see the heightened color in her cheeks. She could just die. How could she be so dumb? He was probably laughing himself sick over her naive reaction.

"You are a class-A idiot," she said. "The man is drop-dead gorgeous, but you don't have to act like a teenager with a crush. Besides, he's looking for a wife to watch those children. With a history of marrying for expediency, what else could you expect?"

Not that she was interested in marriage. She had a

career to build. She wanted to become secure in her life, prove to herself and the world that she could take care of herself and make a difference. It would be a long time before she was interested in marriage.

When Cassandra slipped beneath the covers, she couldn't help but remember the big bed in Jared's room. Knowing he slept on the left side seemed very intimate. She bet no one else in the entire firm knew that about him. Maybe what she said hadn't been so bad. Maybe she could keep working for Hunter Associates. She wasn't sure she could live with Jared withdrawal.

Someone had heard her plea, she thought the next morning when she overheard two fellow employees mention that Jared would be absent yet again. They commiserated with his difficulties in finding competent domestic help. While sorry he hadn't found a baby-sitter, Cassandra was grateful for the respite. At least she didn't have to face him at work after her embarrassing remark. With any luck she'd come down with the flu before tomorrow morning and have a good excuse to cancel the weekend.

But Saturday dawned clear and sunny, and despite herself, Cassandra felt wonderful. She had to admit to the excitement that filled her at the thought of spending the weekend with Jared, even going as a baby-sitter for his twins. She knew she'd spend most of the day in his company. And tonight they were going to dinner alone. She felt almost giddy with anticipation.

She packed a dress, one of the few she owned. It looked a lot more feminine than her business suits. She hoped it would be appropriate for the restaurant. With a little lace at the collar and cuffs, it was dressy.

Watching from her window, she spotted the three of them when they turned the corner and walked toward her building. Cassandra knew parking was difficult so close to Coit Tower and wondered how far away he'd had to park. The twins were each clinging to a hand, Ashley talking nonstop. Brittany looked around as if absorbing every new sight.

But Cassandra's gaze stayed on Jared. He looked incredibly sexy in jeans and a dark pullover shirt. His hair was tousled, as if the wind had danced through. He laughed at something Ashley said, and Cassandra's heart clutched. She could look at him all day and never get her fill. Swallowing hard, she wondered if she were out of her mind to spend the weekend with them.

When the bell rang, she opened her door wide.

"Hi," she said. Afraid to meet Jared's eyes after her confession on the phone the other night, she smiled at the twins instead.

"Hi, Cassie." Ashley flung herself at Cassandra, wrapping her arms around her legs. Cassandra stooped and hugged the little girls, first Ashley, then Brittany. That ritual complete, the twins darted into the living room and began exploring.

"Don't touch anything," Jared roared.

Cassandra laughed and met his eyes. "They can't hurt anything here."

"Maybe not, but it's good practice, right?"

She nodded. Her smile began to fade as her awareness of the man in front of her rose.

He stepped closer, his hand cupping the back of her neck. Slowly he smiled that wicked smile. "I might be equally fascinated," he said in a low drawl. His free hand took hers and placed it against his chest.

Cassandra blushed to the roots of her hair as his mouth descended over hers.

CHAPTER SIX

WHEN Jared pulled away, Cassandra kept her eyes closed. She knew she was about to die of embarrassment.

"Cassie?"

His voice should be patented, she thought. If they could bottle it and sell it, someone would make millions.

"What?" She tried to lower her head, her eyes tightly shut, but his finger beneath her chin kept it raised.

"Open your eyes."

She shook her head.

"Why not?" His tone sounded reasonable. Why couldn't she feel reasonable?

"Because if I keep my eyes shut, no one can see me."

He laughed. "Like the girls. I don't want to shatter your beliefs, but I can see you. And feel you."

She opened her eyes and found herself gazing directly into his, only a few inches away. Her hands were pressed against his strong chest. Even through the soft cotton covering him, she could feel the hard muscles, the crinkling of hair.

He leaned closer and whispered in her ear, "I will let you look at my chest if I can look at yours."

Dropping her forehead against his shoulder, Cassandra knew she was lost. There was no way out of this quagmire of embarrassment.

"I might as well die now," she moaned.

His chuckle annoyed her. Was she just someone to amuse him?

"I for one hope you don't. Come on, it's a beautiful day and we have two wild girls to corral and get into the car. It took me fifteen minutes to figure out the baby seats. Trying to get one in while the other is loose becomes a real challenge."

He tilted her face once more, brushed his lips across hers and released her.

"Ashley, Brittany, what are you doing?" Jared called.

"Noffing."

"Oh, dear," Cassandra said, spinning. She knew that tone. *Nothing* always meant something they weren't supposed to be doing. She rushed into her living room, but didn't see them. She moved to the kitchen and stopped in the doorway. Jared pushed against her to peer over her shoulder.

Both twins sat in the middle of the floor, with bread scattered in every direction. Brittany was attempting to spread a huge chunk of butter on one slice, but the cube was entirely too large to fit on one slice of bread even if it had been soft enough to spread. Crumbs scattered as she pushed the butter into the soft center and through to the floor.

"That's naughty." Jared set Cassandra aside and strode into the room, frowning at the girls. He stooped and took the butter gingerly from Brittany's fingers. "I told you not to touch anything, didn't I?"

Both girls nodded solemnly, their eyes wide with apprehension.

"You have made a mess of Cassie's nice kitchen, wasted food and did it all without permission. Pick up the bread, and tell Cassie you're sorry."

Ashley's little face drooped with sadness. "Sorry, Cassie," she said.

Brittany's thumb shot into her mouth, and her eyes filled with tears. "Sorry, Cassie."

"Your daddy is right. That was naughty. I think five minutes of time out is appropriate." She took each child by the hand and drew them to the small table and chairs she used for eating. She placed a child in each chair and admonished them to sit still until the time was up. Turning, she caught Jared dumping the bread in the trash.

"Time out?" he asked, raising one eyebrow.

"They have to sit on those chairs for five minutes, no talking, no getting down and running around." Cassandra reached for the kitchen timer, set it for five minutes and placed it on the table between the girls.

"Remember, no talking until this bell rings. Next time your daddy tells you not to touch anything, you mind him!"

Both girls solemnly nodded, Brittany still sucking her thumb.

Jared followed Cassandra out of the kitchen. "I think they're sorry. Isn't five minutes a bit harsh?" he asked, looking over his shoulder at the forlorn little girls.

She shook her head. "It might seem endless for them at two, but they have to learn to follow your instructions. This wasn't such a big deal. But if you tell them not to play in the street and they disobey, they could be seriously injured or killed. They have to follow your directions."

"I bow to your superior knowledge and experience."

"You're just glad someone else was around to help with the discipline."

"I am. They are so tiny and young."

"But they need guidance and direction. Don't spoil them, Jared."

"I wouldn't think of it. Are you about ready to leave?"

"Yes." Her small case sat by the door.

"Wouldn't your hair be more comfortable if you didn't keep it in that braid?" he asked. "This is the weekend, and we're supposed to be having fun."

Cassandra touched the neat braid. "You don't like it?"

Jared's fingers tangled with hers as he released the band at the base and began to unthread the braid. "I like your hair swirling around your face, resting on your shoulders, looking like a dark cloud with traces of light shining through. And—" he paused and drew her glasses from her nose "—I like you without your glasses."

Cassandra made a grab for the glasses, but he held them out of her reach.

"I need them to see," she protested.

He held them up and looked through them, frowning. "They're not very strong."

She captured them. "They make the difference between blurry and clear for distances."

"But not close up?" he asked, coming nearer.

Stepping back, she shook her head. Jared deliberately took another step forward, almost laughing as she stepped back again. He could advance until she ran into the wall. Then what would she do?

"Jared," she began, raising one hand as if to stop him. The bell sounded on the kitchen timer.

"Daddy!" Ashley hollered.

"Saved by the bell," he murmured, tapping Cassandra on her chin and turning to the twins.

Cassandra took a shaky breath as she watched him walk into the kitchen. Her heart pounded as if she'd been in a race. Her tummy fluttered, and her skin tingled. What if the timer had not rung? Would he have kissed her? She was getting entirely too enchanted with those kisses.

Jared carried her small case when they left the apartment. Cassandra held on to the children. They skipped beside her and chattered about visiting Grandpa.

"Do they understand the concept?" Jared asked.

"I'm sure they don't. They probably think it's his name."

"This is mine." He stopped by a late-model sedan. The rich dark burgundy color was complemented by a pale gray interior. In the back seat were two baby seats. He opened the door and reached for Brittany when Ashley scrambled in. Cassandra made short work of getting the girls settled. Five minutes later they were off.

"Nice car," she murmured, rubbing her fingertips along the velour seat. Soft and pristine. She wondered how long he'd had it.

"I don't use it much. Around town I usually take a cab. But it's great for long trips, comfortable."

"I would have expected a sports car."

"I had one when we first showed a profit. But they take a lot of care to keep them performance tuned. This is more convenient."

"Tell me something about your grandfather," Cassandra said.

"What's to tell? He's eighty-three, a crusty old man. He's lived alone since my grandmother died when my dad was in high school—except for raising me. His house is old and doesn't have much to recommend it."

"But he's family," she said softly. "I bet he'll be crazy about these little girls."

"Maybe. He's going to be surprised."

"As you were. Did you ever find a reason your wife didn't tell you about them?"

"None that is conclusive. She didn't leave a letter confessing all, if that's what you mean. But her attorney suggested she was afraid I'd insist she stay home and play mommy instead of working. Helen thinks that's probably the case, as well. MaryEllen was obsessed with the business world. She wanted to become a big player in a big field."

"And what do you want, Jared?"

"I want to have a successful company. I enjoy the challenge of getting new business and keeping it. But Hunter Associates is already doing great. I don't want to grow so large I lose all control."

"What else do you want to do with life?"

He flicked her a look then returned his attention to the road. "Funny you should ask that. A month ago I would have said more of the same. But with MaryEllen dying so unexpectedly and finding out I'm a father, I've been doing some thinking. I'm not sure what I want, but my life has already changed tremendously. I'm thinking of finding a nice house for the girls, investing in college accounts. What do you want?"

"A chance to be myself. I love working at Hunter Associates. I'm doing a good job with my accounts, and the GlobalNet project is tremendous. I expect to pull off a stellar success. Then I want to discuss a serious increase in responsibilities and salary."

He laughed. "Always with an eye to the main chance."

"Isn't that the business way?"

"What about your personal life? I take it you don't have a serious relationship going."

He'd kissed her silly more times than she could keep track of and he only brought that up now?

"No, I don't."

"No distractions while you work your way to the top?"

"Something like that."

Brittany demanded a story, and Cassandra was relieved to turn in her seat to comply. It ended the uncomfortable trend of their conversation.

It was after noon by the time they reached Sonora. They'd had to stop twice for rest breaks and to give the girls a few minutes to run around. The awkward tension eased, and Cassandra relaxed and began to enjoy herself. She'd never been in this part of the state and was fascinated to see how different the Sierra Nevada mountains were from the barren mountains around Los Angeles. Tall pines and firs soared toward a crystalline blue sky. The air was redolent with the scent of the cedar and pines—fresh and clean.

Jared turned into a long graveled driveway and stopped near an old house. It needed paint but looked in good repair except for that.

An old man came to the door, peering out to see who had arrived. His face softened when he recognized Jared.

"Hello, Grandpa." Jared greeted the older man, then turned to open the car door. He unfastened Brittany while Cassandra released Ashley from the other side. He wondered what the old man would think of his daughters. Suddenly proud of them, he wanted his grandfather to love them as much as he did.

He took Brittany in his arms, picked up the big white bag from the seat, turned and walked toward the house. "I hope it was all right to drop by. I should have called."

Cassandra followed him, watching avidly as the older man looked at Jared, then the two girls and finally her.

"This is your home, boy, come any time. I see you brought guests. Howdy, ma'am."

"This is Cassandra Bowles. She works for me. Cassie, my grandfather, Silas Hunter," Jared said. "And these two young ladies are Ashley and Brittany Hunter. My daughters."

The old man started, then gazed fiercely at the little girls. "Looks like you might have mentioned something before today," he said gruffly.

"I only found out myself a week ago. Let's go inside and I'll explain everything. We stopped at the burger place in town and brought lunch. I hope you haven't eaten." Jared lifted the bag.

"Not yet. Come in, Miss Bowles."

"Cassandra, please," she said, stepping onto the porch and putting Ashley down.

"Or Cassie, like we call her," Jared said.

The two little girls cautiously entered the dark house.

"Now you young 'uns don't be getting into anything," Grandpa admonished.

They looked at him with wide eyes and didn't move.

"Hmm. I think I have the blocks your daddy played with when he was a little boy. Where did I put them?"

By the time lunch had ended the girls seemed right at home with Silas Hunter. As Cassandra had predicted, he was charmed with the twins.

"I thought I'd take Cassie to Columbia. She's never been to the gold country before," Jared said. "The girls need to nap. Can I leave them with you while we go?"

"I don't know anything about watching little girls. Boys I could handle."

Cassandra smiled. "They don't need much watching

when they sleep. And you've been perfect with them so far. I think they are delighted with their great-grandfather."

"Never thought I'd see the day. Not after that dang fool marriage of yours. I guess it wasn't always platonic."

Jared looked uncomfortable but shrugged, obviously used to his grandfather's blunt ways. Once the girls were asleep, he and Cassandra took off.

Cassandra thoroughly enjoyed her afternoon in Columbia. Fascinated by the old town, she stopped to read every placard and asked innumerable questions. Surprisingly, Jared seemed to know the answer to every one.

"How do you know so much, or are you making it up?" she asked.

He laughed and threaded his fingers through hers, pulling her to the next historical sign. "I grew up around here, remember. You can't live in the gold country without absorbing the history. The California gold rush was one of the largest migration of people in history. Men came from all over the world in hopes of finding color. And I have to admit, it is just as fascinating today as it was when I was growing up. I used to hike down to the Stanislaus River and pan for gold hoping to find a huge nugget or maybe a lost vein somewhere."

"Did you ever get any color?" she asked, feeling almost like a true Argonaut using the jargon.

"A few flakes. I still have them in a jar at Grandpa's. Not enough to set the world on fire."

"Could we go panning?"

"Sure, there's a place here in town. They salt the sand, charge tourists a few bucks and everyone is guaranteed to find some gold."

"I'd rather take the chance in the river."

"We'll do it some day. Maybe we'll still find the mother lode. What would you do with a ton of money?"

"Start my own business," Cassandra said promptly. Then she looked up. "Oh, not that I don't love working at Hunter Associates. But I'd like to be running things one day."

"What would you change about the company if you could?" he asked as if truly interested.

"I don't know enough about the entire setup to suggest any major changes. I know I have a lot to learn. But I have ideas and want to see how they work at some point. It will be years before I'm ready to run an organization. But if I came into a gold mine, then I could hire competent help like you do."

"So you'd be my competition."

Cassandra stopped and thought about it for a moment. "I guess so, in a way. But by the time I'm ready to do anything, Hunter Associates will be a huge firm and I'll start small—going for the little guys who can't afford you."

"Sentiment like that won't make you big bucks."

"But money isn't that important—just knowing you can do the job is what counts. Don't you think?"

"I work for a number of reasons. Money is one of them. But the satisfaction I get is a greater one," Jared admitted.

"But you still want that gold mine?" Cassandra teased.

"Yeah, I still do."

Cassandra didn't get her dinner out that night. When they reached Silas's home, he'd already started a huge pot of beef stew. When he learned of their plans he

looked so crestfallen that Cassandra immediately told
Jared they should eat with him and the girls.

"But I planned to take you to the hotel. They have
wonderful food and a small combo on the weekends for
dancing."

"Take her another time, boy. I want to hear more
about what's going on in your life and what you're planning to do with these young 'uns," Silas said. "Besides,
it's one thing to watch these angels while they sleep. I
suspect they are as full of mischief as you were at that
age when awake."

"Tell him about the makeup," Cassandra suggested,
settling in one of the comfortable chairs. She felt wonderful. The afternoon had passed so swiftly she could
hardly believe it. It was because of her companion, she
knew. He'd been attentive and informative and fun. And
she'd discovered a bit more about her boss. Jared was a
fascinating man.

"It's all tied in with trying to get a baby-sitter," Jared
began.

Silas chuckled at the antics of the twins and twice
threw speculative glances at Cassandra. "Looks to me
like you ought to think about getting married again," he
said when Jared finished.

She pretended to not notice. The last thing she needed
was for Jared to get the idea that she would be the perfect wife. He'd mentioned it a couple of times—always
right after she had helped with the twins.

Dinner was lively. The girls constantly tried to dom-
inate the conversation. They were intrigued with the
older man and loved chatting with him. He nodded and
smiled and acted as if he understood every word. They
were enchanted. When the dishes had been washed and
put away, without the girls' help this time, they all sat

in the living room. Brittany snuggled into Jared's lap and Ashley hesitated, torn between her newly discovered great-grandfather and Cassie. Finally, she wandered to Cassie and raised her arms.

"Up."

Cassandra pulled her into her lap and hugged her. These girls were so precious. For a moment she gave a thought to their mother. MaryEllen would miss so much.

"That tale you told earlier about the makeup reminded me of the time you got into the honey, remember?" Silas said, leaning back in his chair, a look of amusement covering his face.

"No need to rake up old stories, Grandpa," Jared said hastily.

Cassandra laughed. "We girls would love to hear it, wouldn't we, Ashley?"

When she nodded vigorously, Silas began telling tales about Jared as a little boy. It was obvious the girls weren't too sure who the little boy was. They kept looking at their father. He was so big, it must be impossible for them to imagine him as a small child.

Cassandra reveled in each story, intrigued with the glimpses into Jared's past. His life had been quite different from hers. He'd found love and security with his grandfather. He was so lucky. She had a box full of mementos from various homes and her cherished dolly—that was all. No one to sit with and reminisce. The conversation centered around Jared's antics as a boy, and from the fond way his grandfather told the tales, the old man clearly loved his only grandson.

When Brittany fell asleep in his arms, Jared rose to put her to bed. "I'll be back for that one," he said.

Cassandra started to rise, but Silas shook his head. When Jared had left, he turned to her. "Let him do it. I wanted a chance to talk with you, and this is probably the only one I'll get. Never saw my boy so attentive to someone before. He never lets you take six steps away.''

Cassandra flushed. "I don't think that's quite so. I'm here to help with the girls.''

"It's about the girls, I'm thinking. He needs a wife. Someone to help him raise these young 'uns. You seem to know what you're doing. Ever have children?''

"In a manner of speaking. I watched children while I was growing up—after school, weekends, nights.''

"Mmm, it shows. You've got a good touch with these little girls. From what I heard today, better even than their mother.'' He shook his head. "Dang fool idea marrying to start a business. Yet it seemed to work. The firm is doing well, if Jared's reports are true. But now Jared needs someone to show him how to make a family. We didn't have a normal one. No woman in the place.'' Silas chuckled suddenly. "That's sure not the case now—he's already outnumbered. A wife would only add to the female majority.''

Cassandra smiled politely. "Don't you think Jared should marry for love?'' she asked. "Not just to acquire another wife?''

"Don't know if it'll ever happen. Sometimes being a good companion is all you can expect. I had that with Emma. Jared's father fell in love with his wife and they fought like cats and dogs. Don't know that I believe in it for a marriage. More important things come into play.''

Cassandra felt Ashley fall asleep, her body suddenly limp and heavy. She cuddled her closer, breathing in her sweet baby scent. Maybe Jared could be excused for his first marriage, if his grandfather's advice was anything to go by. But he would be doing himself and his new wife a disservice if he married again without love. Did he even know what it was? How to display it?

Of course he did. He was loving and devoted to his children—and he'd learned of their existence less than two weeks ago.

For a second she wished he'd show her the same affection, come to care for her as strongly as he obviously cared for his daughters. But she knew the folly of such wishful thinking.

"One down, now for number two," Jared said, crossing the room to lift Ashley from Cassandra's lap. His dark eyes gazed into hers, and she almost lifted her hand to his cheek. Clenching her fingers, she looked away, right into the wise eyes of Silas Hunter. He looked quickly at his grandson and then gazed into space, but Cassandra wasn't fooled. The old man wanted something to develop between them. It didn't matter to him if they loved one another. He wanted someone to help his grandson.

Jared hesitated in the doorway. The girls were both sound asleep. It was still early enough that he and Cassandra could run down to the hotel and have dessert, maybe dance for a while. Except for the plane ride to New York and the afternoon in Columbia, they'd never spent any time together without the girls. He'd looked forward to this evening. She'd left her hair down after he'd released it that morning. In the afternoon's sun it had glowed like rich ebony. She looked young and carefree and delighted with every tidbit he shared. Soaking up the folklore from gold rush days, she'd questioned him incessantly. Just like the twins did. Only he had an easier time talking with Cassandra.

Easier than with most of the women he knew.

Watching her from the shadows in the hall, he wondered why. She chatted with his grandfather. He could hear the murmur of their voices, but not the words. From the comments his not-so-sly grandfather made, Jared knew Silas thought Cassandra would make the perfect wife for a widower with two small children.

Sometimes Jared thought so himself. Would she consent to marry him? It would solve so many problems if she'd marry him and be a stay-at-home wife. He shook his head. To look at, she seemed like the perfect mate, sweet and docile. But he knew she'd never agree to such a plan. Her career was too important to her.

His eyes hardened. How did women put mere business ahead of caring for their children? Wasn't there joy and excitement in raising a child? Shaping how she would face the future? First MaryEllen, now Cassandra. Neither wanted to raise children. Each wanted to make it in business.

Yet didn't he want the same thing? He didn't plan to stay home with the children. It was the old double standard, and in an instant he realized how Cassandra felt. But even if she didn't stay home, she would be there in the evenings, giving advice, telling him how to handle discipline and giving the girls a different perspective. Children needed a mother and a father. It was up to him to provide both for his twins.

"Are they asleep?" Cassandra asked when he stepped into the living room.

"Never even stirred when I put them in their pajamas. I think they'll sleep through until morning." He looked at Silas. "It's still early. Would you watch them while Cassandra and I head for town?"

"Sure. Asleep I can handle them."

"How about it, Cassie, want to go out for dessert?"

"I don't know, Jared. I thought we could sit here and have Silas share more of his memories. Think of the blackmail I can use with all I'm learning," she teased.

"I can see I have to get a vow of silence from you before we leave," Jared replied, sitting on the chair opposite her. "It's still warm out. Want to go for a walk?"

"That I'd like." Cassandra jumped up. "We'll be back soon, Silas. Dust off all those old stories."

Cassandra stopped abruptly on the porch. Jared ran into her. "Whoops," he said, stopping suddenly. "What's wrong?"

"It's so dark here. In the city there are streetlights, lights from all the buildings. It's black as pitch here!"

"Give your eyes a chance to get used to the dark. The stars provide light. And once the moon gets above the trees, we'll be able to see fine. I know my way around, Cassie. Come on." He took her hand in his, threaded his fingers through hers and stepped off the porch. Walking in the center of the graveled drive, Jared kept his pace slow to make it easier on Cassie. She wasn't as high as his shoulder. Her stride was short.

"It's quiet here, too," she murmured as they strolled down the drive. When they reached the country road, he turned left. "It must have been so much fun to grow up here. Did you have a tree fort?"

"Sure. And swings hanging from tree limbs. We used to swim at one of the creeks that feed the Stan."

"No wonder you want to get a house with a yard for your girls."

"And a mother." Jared stopped and pulled Cassie in front of him. His hands rested on her shoulders as he lowered his head, trying to see her in the dim light.

"Will you provide them with that, Cassie? Will you marry me?"

CHAPTER SEVEN

CASSANDRA stared at him in dawning horror. She pulled free, turned and walked briskly along the path they'd just taken. She'd run if she could. Instead she had to settle for furiously stomping, trying to see in the faint illumination from the stars.

"Cassie, wait a minute." Jared grasped her arm and halted her. His grip tightened.

"At least discuss it," he said.

"What's to discuss? I won't be a baby-sitter for the rest of my life. I spent a lot of time and effort to get a business degree so I could move beyond that. I want to use it."

"I never said you couldn't use your degree, that I didn't want you to work. But you're so good with the girls. They like you. You like them. It would be the perfect solution."

"For you, maybe. I don't see it in any way perfect."

"You want to get married some day, don't you? Most women do. We get along. We had a good time today—"

"Jared, stop. Just because we had fun one afternoon doesn't mean we're suited for *marriage*. Listen to yourself. You couldn't even make a pretense of wanting me for myself. All you want is a mother for the girls. A woman doesn't want to be married unless she's loved and cherished. Or at the very least appreciated for herself. We don't even know each other."

"You've worked for me for two years. I know how you are in the office, and these last couple of weeks,

I've seen how you are with the girls. We have the foundation for a strong marriage. And I've never lied to you. Did you want me to fall on my knees and declare my undying love?'' His scathing tone displayed his feelings.

''No. You wouldn't mean it.''

''You're right. I don't believe in love, at least not the fairy-tale version. But we could build a good life together. Don't say no tonight, Cassie. Think about it.''

''I don't need to think about it. I—'' Before Cassandra could finish her sentence, Jared covered her mouth with his. It was as if she had been waiting especially for his touch. Her lips parted, and he took advantage, tracing the soft flesh with his tongue, slipping inside to sip of her sweetness. He moved his hands to the silky softness of her hair, to hold her firm and positioned for his kiss. He forgot the burden of becoming a sudden father, forgot about the demands of the office. The only reality was the petite woman in his arms and the fire her kisses fed.

At last he pulled back and gazed at her bemused expression. A skilled negotiator, Jared knew when to keep silent. He wanted her and he intended to have her. But sometimes pushing too hard could kill a deal. He'd coax her, cajole her and bribe her, if need be. But he wanted her for the mother of his daughters, and he'd make sure he got her.

''Let's return to the house. I don't think you want a walk,'' he said, releasing her. ''We'll talk more about this later.'' He was careful to stay near but did not touch her on the walk back. The light on the porch beckoned, and Cassandra increased her pace when she saw it.

''I don't need to talk further,'' she said as she mounted the steps to the wide porch. She'd kept quiet on the walk, too stunned at the turn of events to marshal her thoughts. But she wanted to make her position clear before retiring for the night.

"And I won't take no for an answer tonight. Go on inside, I still want a walk." Jared waited until she was at the door, then spun and headed toward the road.

Cassandra watched him stride away, her heart fluttering wildly in her chest. His kiss had been devastating. She would have fallen in a heap if he hadn't been holding her. Her knees had felt like marshmallows. Lightly she brushed her warm lips with her fingertips. If she was foolish enough to ever entertain his notion of marriage, she'd be entitled to kisses like that all the time. With a quiet groan, she opened the door. She'd never get anything done if that were the case. Jared's kisses disturbed her too much to promote clear thinking.

Cassandra spent some time visiting with Silas. He spoke of Sonora and the changes he'd seen in the sleepy little gold rush town during the years he'd lived there. Before long his eyes began to droop, and Cassandra knew he was growing tired.

"I think I'll just slip on to bed, if that's all right," she said, standing. When he nodded, she crossed the hall to the spare room that had been assigned to her. The bed was not large, but more than ample. She was glad she'd brought a sturdy cotton nightgown. The evenings in the mountains were cool.

Turning off the lights a little while later, Cassandra lay awake in the dark listening for Jared's step. She tried to ignore the churning of her senses as she relived his proposal. No mention of love or devotion. Simply that his girls needed a mother and he wanted her for the job. Was that how he saw a wife—as someone to fill a position like any employee?

She wanted to be angry at the callous way he phrased

things. But she couldn't help imagining being married to him. Seeing him every day and every night. Sharing meals, bath time with the twins and family outings.

She rolled on her side and curled up the way she had as a child. Was she foolish to pass up his proposal? She'd admired him since the day they'd met. Since finding out his wife had died, her feelings had become stronger. Not that admiration was a foundation for marriage. Ever since her mother had died, she'd searched for love. Should she settle for anything less?

What would happen when she refused? He'd turn to someone else, of course. His interest in her was tied to the twins. He'd never looked at her twice before insisting she accompany him on the trip to New York, and she'd only been pressed into service for that journey because she had crucial experience.

In all fairness, she had to admit, prior to that he'd been a married man. He was too honorable to have shown any interest in a woman not his wife. Given the circumstances of his marriage, she thought even more highly of him that he had not sought other women.

Would he be as loyal to her as he had been to MaryEllen? How could he propose another business affair? But then, from the stories she'd heard tonight about his childhood, what did Jared know about a family? His parents had evidently fought every moment of their marriage. When they died, he'd moved in with his crusty old grandfather. Silas had admitted his wife had been the primary parent with their son. He'd had limited experience when it came to raising Jared.

Cassandra smiled in the dark. She thought the old man had done a wonderful job. Jared was kind and considerate. A bit arrogant and demanding, but that could be excused or worked around. The honesty and honor that shone so strongly were not traits to be learned, but innate.

She could do worse.

What was she doing, considering his ludicrous proposal?

Couldn't she do better? Couldn't she find a man who loved her? She had to refuse Jared. Her career was important. And somewhere, some time, there would be someone who loved her.

The steps in the hall were quiet, but Cassandra recognized them. Jared was safe at home. Curiously content, she drifted to sleep.

The next morning Cassandra came awake when her door opened. Two thumping sets of feet crossed the room, and two small bodies flung themselves against the side of her bed. Opening her eyes slowly, she gazed into identical sunny faces.

"Hi, there," Cassandra said, smiling. They looked adorable.

"Hi, Cassie. Up?" Ashley held up her arms.

"Me, too," said Brittany.

Cassandra drew both girls into the bed, snuggling one on either side of her. Their bare feet were freezing. She tucked the blankets around the three of them and settled against the pillow, her heart singing.

"Tell us a story," Ashley demanded.

Cassandra hid a smile. The child sounded just as imperious as her father. Her heart filled with love for these precious twin girls. They looked so alike yet were so different.

"How about Jack and the Beanstalk?" Cassandra asked. She launched into the tale, stretching out scenes, using a gruff voice for the giant, saying, "Fee, fie, fo, fum." They watched her with rapt attention, giggling at

the silly parts, looking mesmerized when the giant began
to pursue Jack.

"Isn't that a little scary for two-year-olds?" Jared
asked from the door.

Cassandra looked up, startled. She'd been so en-
grossed in entertaining the girls she hadn't heard him.
He'd dressed in jeans and a blue cotton shirt. His shoulder propped against the doorjamb, he crossed his arms
and watched them.

"It's just a fairy tale. All of them are a bit gruesome
and violent. But didn't you hear them when you were
little?"

He nodded. "But I was a boy."

"As if that makes a difference."

"Hi, Daddy." Ashley waved. "We snuggle wif
Cassie."

"I see you two are snuggled with Cassie. Is there
room for me?"

Cassandra's gaze flew to his as color stained her
cheeks. "No, there is not room for you."

"It is a small bed. My king-size bed at home would
hold all of us easily."

Cassandra remembered the huge bed that dominated
his bedroom, the tousled covers and the indented left
pillow. She could sleep on the right side, and when the
girls wakened they could join them, snuggling beneath
the covers for more storytelling. The image was so
sharp, Cassandra thought she could reach out and touch
it. Longing rose. She could have that life if she just said
yes.

"Time to get up. Grandpa's making flapjacks," Jared
said, eyeing her quizzically.

"What's fap jack?" Brittany asked, pulling her thumb
from her mouth.

"Pancakes, baby girl, the best this side of the Mississippi."

"Well, that frame of reference will help these two," Cassandra said, wishing Jared would leave. How was she to get out of bed with him standing there watching every move?

He smiled and remained standing exactly where he was.

"Want to get the girls dressed first?" she asked.

"No. I shudder to think how much syrup they'll spill on themselves. We can give them a quick bath after breakfast, throw the nightgowns in the laundry. Did you bring a robe?"

Cassandra nodded. Not that she had any intention of sitting in her nightgown and robe and eating breakfast while Jared was fully dressed and looking as sexy as could be.

"I'd rather dress before breakfast," she said primly.

"Now, why am I not surprised? Hurry up, then, Grandpa already has the first batch in the pan."

The girls scooted from the bed and raced out the door.

"Get something on their feet. They were like ice when they climbed in with me," Cassandra said, sitting up, holding the blanket. She felt as shy as a Victorian maiden, but there was no way she was getting out of bed with Jared standing there watching her.

"Need help?"

She glared at him. He knew! Darn him.

"Go help your daughters."

Laughing softly, he pushed away from the door frame. But he didn't head for the kitchen. He stepped into her room, immediately displacing all the air. Cassandra watched, mesmerized, as he slowly crossed the small space to her bed. He looked like some sleek predatory animal ready to pounce. Her heart pounded. She couldn't breathe. Her fingers clutched the blanket tightly while she watched his every move. She didn't trust that gleam in his eyes. She didn't trust him at all!

"Good morning," he said, and leaned over to kiss her.

Cassandra didn't know how her face tilted to his. She closed her eyes and felt as if she were floating. She was pressed against the pillows before she could draw a breath. And when she did, Jared flooded her senses. How did her arms find their way around his neck? How could she be holding on so tightly? She didn't want to encourage the man! He had enough dangerous ideas without her contributing to them.

"Jared!" Silas roared from the kitchen. "Breakfast is on the table."

"Uh-oh." Jared pulled away and sat on the edge of the bed, his fingers brushing the tangle of dark hair on the pillow. "That's his get-in-here-this-minute voice. I remember it well from when I was growing up."

"Don't you think you'd better go?" Cassandra wanted to throw herself into his arms and have him kiss her again. Her heated blood rushed through her veins. She could scarcely breathe, and she was practically asking him to stay.

"Are you getting up?"

"Yes, after you leave." She drew the covers higher and glared at him. "You should not be here!" It was too little, too late, but she tried to draw on some modicum of common sense and practicality.

"I like it here. I like being around you," he said, grinning audaciously.

"The answer is still no!" Defiant, she refused to be cajoled into agreeing to his outrageous proposal.

"I don't remember asking any question."

"The one from last night."

"Ah, that one. I don't want to discuss that yet. Maybe later. Just keep an open mind."

"No. I've told you the answer already."

"Cassandra, you're new at negotiating. You haven't heard all the points yet. There is always a price. I just have to find yours." He took her hand and held it in his, studying it, tracing the soft skin with a fingertip.

"Now you make me sound like a piece of furniture. You're planning to buy me?"

"Maybe bribe?"

Six kisses a day would probably do it, her traitorous mind thought.

Gathering her dignity, she withdrew her hand. "If you would let me have a little privacy, I'd get up and dressed."

"Don't get dressed on my account."

"You're dressed."

"I can change that." He reached for the top button of his shirt.

"No!" She closed her eyes tightly. "Go eat breakfast."

The bed shifted when he rose, and she heard his chuckle as he walked away. He could be very aggravating.

She opened her eyes, flung the covers off, got up, snatched her clothes and headed for the bathroom. The sooner they ate and got on the road, the sooner she'd be home, safe and sound.

And alone.

"I'm not getting married to be a surrogate mother!" she said. She brushed her hair until it shone. Satisfied she looked her best in the comfortable jeans and jonquil-yellow shirt, she tossed her nightgown in the bedroom and hurried to the kitchen. No sense abusing Silas's hospitality because of her annoyance with Jared.

"Sleep good?" Silas asked when she appeared in the doorway.

"Great." Ignoring Jared, she took the seat the older man indicated and looked at the stack of pancakes on her plate. "I can't eat all this." Did Silas think she was a lumberjack? There must have been eight or nine huge pancakes.

"Eat what you want. The rest we'll throw out for the birds," Jared said.

"We have fap jacks," Brittany said. A trail of glistening syrup on her chin and the front of her nightie indicating she'd started eating.

"They're very good," Ashley said around a mouthful.

"Swallow before talking," Cassandra said softly, then darted a glance at Jared. She'd spoken before thinking. Acting just like a mother. She didn't like the smug expression on his face. He was driving her crazy. She'd said no a half dozen times. Wasn't he listening?

Cassandra ate quickly, hoping they could head for home soon. It had been a mistake to come for the weekend. She needed distance and the sanctity of her apartment to gather her defenses. And she needed to stay away from Jared. The man wouldn't listen to her. Kissed her whenever it suited him. And she'd told him no. Well, maybe she hadn't told him not to kiss her again, she admitted. But surely he knew they had no future together.

He should be out looking for another woman to become the mother of his children.

The thought hit her. If he found someone else, he'd never kiss her again. Wouldn't call her to help with Ashley or Brittany. Another woman would be charmed by the twins, laugh at their antics, have her heart melt when Brittany snuggled close and smiled in quiet happiness.

Cassandra would have her career. Somehow the excitement had faded. She needed to get home to regain her perspective.

But Jared was in no hurry. Once the girls were cleaned up and dressed, they went outside. He insisted Cassandra join them, then had her suggest the games they play.

"You know what children like," he said, reinforcing her belief he saw her as a child-care specialist only.

The day was beautiful. The sun shone in a cloudless sky. A slight breeze brought the scent of cedar and pine. Warmth from the sun's rays kept them comfortable. A change from the briskness in the air last night.

With the intent of giving them plenty of exercise before the long car ride, Cassandra suggested red light, green light. The girls did their best. If they didn't always stop at red light, no one seemed to care. Laughing and giggling, they ran fast to reach their daddy, who was it. After several sets, they switched to follow the leader. Ashley insisted Cassie lead them. Cassandra hopped, watching as the twins did their best to copy her. Then she pirouetted, then skipped. She ran slowly, then stopped abruptly. Both girls careered into her, then Jared followed.

They all tumbled to the ground, laughing and squirming. In a flash both girls were on their feet. "That's fun!" Ashley said, beaming at the two adults still on the ground.

"Yeah, well, I wasn't expecting your father," Cassandra said, sitting.

Jared lay back, stacked his hands and rested his head

on them. "I haven't played games like these in more than twenty-five years."

"You never lose your touch. Were you always this klutzy?" she asked, looking at him. He'd closed his eyes, turned his face toward the sun. His skin was already tanned, taut over high cheekbones. Cassandra wished she dared trace the outlines of his face, feel that warm skin, test the closeness of his shave.

Brittany plopped down beside Jared. "No nap," she said, poking him.

He smiled and opened one eye. "Not napping, just resting."

"Daddy's really old. He needs to rest after he plays," Cassandra said.

"Witch," he said without heat. "You'll have them believing that."

"Daddy old," Brittany yelled to Ashley. Then she scrambled to her feet and went to see what her twin was doing. Pulling up dandelions, as far as Cassandra could tell. She watched them to make sure they didn't put the flowers in their mouths.

"Thirty-two is not old."

"If you are two, it is."

"How old are you?"

"Twenty-five."

"It would be a real marriage, Cassie. I want to have more children. You could have your own babies as well as these," Jared said without opening his eyes. "Maybe a few years ahead of what you planned, but so what? That just means they'll be grown and gone earlier. You'll still have many years to build a huge career."

She watched the twins as heat washed through her at his words. Babies with Jared? Maybe a little boy next time? A tough little guy who would like to spend summers visiting with Silas, playing in the mountains, growing up like his daddy.

Cassandra took a shaky breath and stood. "It's getting late. We should pack up and head back. I think we've run them ragged. They'll probably sleep the entire way home."

"Just to be full of pep when we get back, huh?"

Watching as he effortlessly rose, Cassandra couldn't help but notice how well he filled out his jeans, how his shirt emphasized the broadness of his shoulders. He looked serious in his business suits. Casual clothes revealed the tantalizing masculinity of his body. She closed her eyes and turned away.

"Cassie?" Jared came closer.

"What?"

"It's time to discuss this. And I'm willing to throw in something else. Something that I think will appeal to you."

She looked at him and held her breath. He was so dear to her. Suddenly she knew why she wanted him to kiss her, to spend time with her. To want her—not as a mother to his children but for his own personal lover. She loved him! She had admired him for months, reveled in every hint of praise he'd showed her at work, more so than praise from a boss would normally warrant. But these last two weeks had shown her how truly special Jared was. He'd taken a bad blow with the unexpected discovery of the twins. And immediately taken charge. She could tell by watching them that he adored his daughters. She wished he felt some of that same adoration for her.

Her heart pounded. She couldn't marry the man—yet how could she allow him to marry anyone else?

Jared leaned toward her, his eyes searching her face.

Slowly he drew off her glasses and tucked them in his shirt pocket. "Marry me, and I'll throw in twenty percent ownership of Hunter Associates. Your career will be assured forever."

Stunned, she stared at him. For a moment she thought she might faint. The trees and deep blue sky faded to a nondescript gray. She could only focus on his dark eyes and the echo of the words that played in her head.

"What did you say?"

"You heard me, twenty percent. Which isn't all bad considering I only have fifty-one percent. The other forty-nine percent now belongs to Ashley and Brittany. It will still be a family organization. And we can vote their stock for another nineteen years or so. What do you say? Is it enough?"

Tears stung her eyes. She'd just realized she loved the man, and he was bribing her to marry him! Her heart ached.

Gently Jared tucked a strand of hair behind her ear, his fingers lingering a moment longer than necessary, as if he enjoyed the feel of her soft skin. "Just like a marketing analyst to analyze everything to death," he said into the growing silence. "Just say yes, Cassie. Don't look for every possible ramification."

"It'll never work."

"Of course it will work," he said arrogantly. "We'll make sure of it. Say yes!"

Cassandra held her breath, thoughts spinning in her mind. Take a chance. She drew a deep breath and threw caution to the wind. Slowly she nodded.

Jared smiled and leaned forward as if to kiss her. She raised her face. She was probably making the biggest mistake of her life, but recklessly throwing caution to the wind, she promised herself she'd do all she could to make sure it did work.

His breath brushed across her cheeks. Closing her eyes, she waited for his kiss.

"Ashley, no!" Jared's voice roared in her ear. He released her and he darted to the little girl, then he thrust his finger inside her mouth and popped out mangled dandelion petals. He stooped and scolded the child. Cassandra watched, the scene slightly blurry. Engaged eight seconds and already he'd ignored her for his children. Was this a sign of how their life would be? Not if she could help it. But she had better make sure he never suspected she had fallen in love with him. He was just the type to take advantage of that fact.

The drive home was quiet. The twins fell asleep in their baby seats almost as soon as Jared pulled away from his grandfather's house. Silas had packed them a picnic lunch, but Cassandra refused to let Jared waken the girls. They were tired and could use the sleep. And it would make the trip to San Francisco go that much faster.

Her mind spun in a million directions. She had some more work to do on the GlobalNet account before they could begin their preliminary draft. Had Melanie finished her part of the projections? Cassandra would have to check first thing in the morning. After work tomorrow, she needed to get some groceries. She tried to keep her mind from the monumental change she'd agreed to, but she couldn't do so for long.

If they married, she wouldn't need her apartment anymore. Could she get a sublet? The thought crashed into her. She had agreed to marry Jared Hunter! Was she making a mistake? Darting a glance at him, she wondered how soon he'd want to get married. Could she really go through with this?

If she didn't, he'd find someone else. That above all else reinforced her decision.

He flicked a glance at her. "Having second thoughts?" he asked calmly.

"Maybe."

He frowned. "I thought we could be married next Friday. I'll have Helen set things up at the courthouse. We'll get the license one day this week at lunch."

"So soon?" Panic threatened to flare.

"Any reason to wait?" Jared asked reasonably.

Cassandra shook her head. She would get used to this. She hoped.

Jared bypassed her place and drove directly to his. She helped feed the children supper and then bathed them. For a few moments she felt as if she'd been transported back to New York, taking care of the girls, feeling awkward and out of place in the apartment. Only now the routine was growing familiar.

Sweet-smelling and ready for bed, the girls ran to the living room to bounce on the sofa, ready for a story.

"Cassie can tell us the story," Jared said as he scooped up Ashley and held her in his lap. When Cassandra sat, he scooted over until his hip touched hers, his thigh pressed against hers. His look dared her to object.

Scarcely able to breathe, much less concentrate on a story, Cassandra cuddled close with Brittany and held out her hand to Ashley. "Do fee fum," the little girl demanded, placing her hand in Cassandra's and smiling winningly.

Despite their long nap, both girls were nodding by the time Cassandra finished her rendition of Jack and the

Beanstalk. She and Jared carried the twins into their room and tucked them into their cribs. For the first time Cassandra considered what she'd agreed to. She would have an instrumental role in shaping the lives of these precious babies. She'd be the mommy they remembered. She'd be the one to take them to school, attend their Christmas plays, hear their lessons and mop up tears when they were teenagers and boys proved perplexing and disappointing.

And she knew she'd love them both until the day she died. Just as she loved their father.

Turning, she smiled shyly at Jared. "This is the best time."

"They are angels when asleep, aren't they?"

He led the way to the living room. "Are you anxious to be off or can you stay and talk for a few minutes?" he asked.

"I can stay if you want me to," she said.

He studied her. "Sounds like the perfect employee. You're a partner now, Cassie. And in less than a week you'll be my wife."

"And what do you expect of this marriage, Jared? Docility? For me to meekly bow to your will?"

He laughed. "Not from you. I expect you'll do whatever you think is right and let me know somewhere along the way." Unexpectedly his face sobered. He drew her closer and rested his forehead against hers. "I'm expecting a willing wife. A woman who will help me with the children and with the business. I don't expect you to stay at home and devote yourself to Ashley and Brittany. But you'll be here every night and weekends. As much as I will."

"And for yourself?" she asked, wishing he'd stop

talking and just kiss her so soundly she never had another doubt in her life.

"Someone to share things with. Don't run off to New York."

Since she couldn't imagine doing such a thing, Cassandra found it exceedingly easy to promise that. Would her reward for her acquiescence be a kiss? She closed her eyes and shook her head. She was becoming obsessed with his kisses.

Yet, as if he read her mind, he complied.

But this kiss was not a sweet seal to their engagement. It was fiery hot, passionate and exciting. He held her tightly as if there were no one else on the planet. And for a long time, Cassandra forgot that there was.

CHAPTER EIGHT

HELEN displayed no sign of surprise when Jared told her of his engagement the next morning. He realized he had expected some show of astonishment instead of the almost smug expression on her face. Looking at her quizzically, he asked her to step into his office.

"Congratulations. I think it's about time," Helen said as she closed the door behind her.

"About time? MaryEllen hasn't even been dead two months. I'm rushing."

"Time that you found someone to love and marry. You and MaryEllen were too much alike. Of course I know you two married to build the company. Time you had a wife for yourself this time. It isn't as if you and MaryEllen even lived together over the last three years. Be happy, boss, and don't worry about it."

Jared opened his mouth to clear up Helen's misconception, then snapped it shut. If she wanted to think this was a love match, who was he to burst her bubble? At least Cassie knew the truth. He frowned and moved to sit behind his desk. At least he thought she did. She had mentioned love yesterday. But Jared knew love was some nebulous emotion that supposedly bound people together. A marriage could succeed well without it when the partners respected each other and had similar goals.

Anxious to get to work, he began to list the tasks he had for Helen. Once he had the wedding behind him, he could concentrate on business.

"And how does Cassandra feel about this?" Helen asked when he paused.

"She agreed to marry me," he said. A feeling of complacency filled him. She had agreed. And he wouldn't let her change her mind.

"I don't mean about that, I mean about all your plans for the wedding. Usually the bride decides these things."

He frowned. "I don't know."

"A word of advice, boss. At least ask."

"Call her in," he ordered.

Cassandra entered Jared's office in response to Helen's request. She looked first at Jared, then at Helen. Was this some kind of meeting?

"Congratulations and best wishes," Helen said, smiling warmly.

Cassandra smiled back, feeling nervous. The more she thought about this, the more nervous she grew. Yet knowing how she felt about Jared, she could not stand aside and let someone else marry him and share a life with him and the twins. She wanted that for herself.

"I've asked Helen to make arrangements for the ceremony. She'll reserve a room at City Hall on Friday and find out what we need to do for a license."

"Actually, Jared, we need to talk about this some more," Cassandra said as she sat in one of the chairs near the desk.

"What's there to talk about? You agreed to marry me, that's the end of it."

She shook her head. "No, it's the beginning. But that's not what I mean. After I got home last night, I began to think. This is my only wedding. I don't want some hurried affair at City Hall."

He leaned back in amazement. "You aren't going to

tell me you want some full-blown wedding that takes six months or longer to plan?"

"No. It's not like I have a big family or anything. But I do have some good friends whom I'd want to attend. And I expect you have some friends who should be there, and your grandfather. I want a church wedding. I thought maybe we could have the ceremony at a little chapel near Columbus. If Helen wouldn't mind seeing if we could use it Friday, we could still meet your schedule. But I'm not getting married at City Hall."

"How many friends are you talking about?" he asked suspiciously.

"I want the members of my team to be invited. And I have several neighbors to ask. And my friend Susie can stand up with me. About ten in all."

"Ten." He stared at her. He had not expected this. A quick ceremony to make it legal was all he anticipated. It was what he and MaryEllen had done. Now Cassandra was talking like a real bride. Which, of course, she was. For a moment, Jared really looked at her. He wondered if he'd done the right thing for Cassie in insisting she marry him. She was young, had her whole life ahead of her. Was it fair to tie her to a man who already had two children, who had one business marriage behind him? Would she grow to resent him as the years rolled by?

The image of the twins arose. They had a new baby-sitter today, Jennifer McConnall. Helen had seen to that. But how long before she left? The girls needed stability and love. Cassie would provide both. And he would do anything to insure his daughters got the best.

"There are several people who would be quite upset if Jared had a wedding and didn't invite them," Helen added.

"I don't need your input," he snapped.

"Sure you do," Cassandra said. "If she's the wedding coordinator, we both need to listen to her. So how many should we plan from Jared's side?" she asked Helen.

"His senior management staff, his attorney and several friends from the various organizations he belongs to. Whomever he asks to be best man. Add his grandfather and we are probably talking at least a dozen or more."

"That'd be more than two dozen at the ceremony," he said.

"He's always so good with numbers, isn't he?" Cassandra said proudly. "What's the matter with that? And don't forget the girls. They have to be there."

"They're babies. They don't belong at a wedding."

"Yes, they do. They have to be there." Cassandra refused to get ruffled, though his dark look had her heart racing. She'd considered things long and hard last night. If she was to be coerced into a marriage of convenience—Jared's convenience—she insisted on having a say in things. *Start as you mean to go on,* her foster mother had often said.

Jared stared at her for a long moment, then nodded. "Do as the bride says, Helen."

The week flew by. Cassandra agonized over her agreement to this marriage every moment. Was she doing the right thing?

Distracted by her thoughts, she was constantly teased into paying attention by her team members. Awed at first by her forthcoming marriage to the boss, everyone soon settled into a routine when they saw she made no changes in her demeanor. Cassandra was not a person to put on airs. Besides, the entire situation seemed like some dream. How could she believe it, much less act on it?

When Jared suggested she move into the office near his, she declined. For the time being, she was a marketing analyst, and at work, at least, she didn't want any favors for being the boss's wife.

"You're also part owner now, which makes you the boss," he said on Wednesday when she protested the move.

"After the wedding, and then only on paper. Compared to you and the other senior managers, I know so little. It will be years before I'll be ready to make major decisions. Maybe we should hold off on my getting shares."

"Hold off?" Jared stared at her in confusion. "The shares were what changed your mind. What do you mean, hold off? You're not trying to delay the wedding, are you?"

Exasperated, she shook her head. "No, I'm not trying to delay anything—except putting shares in my name. I'd thought you'd be happy about that."

He narrowed his eyes. They were in his office to discuss how to present the GlobalNet preliminary analysis in the best light. When he made a casual mention of her part ownership, Cassandra had to say something. She felt a tremendous amount of guilt at the thought of taking the shares.

"I thought that was what tipped the scales so you said yes," he said thoughtfully.

She swallowed and looked at the notes on the sheet before her. She could hardly tell him she was marrying him to make sure no one else did. He'd want to know why, and that she couldn't tell him.

"I just think we should wait, that's all."

"All right. You let me know," he said. In seconds, he was back into the GlobalNet project.

*   *   *

By Friday morning, Cassandra was a nervous wreck. She'd packed enough clothes to cover any and all circumstances for the weekend. She'd have to come back and finish packing. Arrangements had been made to have her furniture stored or disposed of. The apartment was on the market. She hoped someone wanted it right away.

During the week, she had done her best to ignore the coming change in her life. But at the oddest times, she'd remember Jared's words in the meadow at his grandfather's. *This would be a real marriage.* Of course he'd want that. He planned to stay married for the rest of his life, and he was too virile to settle for some platonic relationship. Then her thoughts would turn to the bed she'd seen in his apartment. Trying to imagine them together in it would cause a warm flush to invade her body. Doubts would then spring up, and she'd wonder if she could go through with the wedding.

On Friday morning, as she was dressing, she still worried about whether she was doing the right thing.

"Cassandra, are you all right?" Susie asked. Her friend was wearing a rose suit that suited her dark coloring.

Cassandra blinked. She was dreaming again. She smiled at her friend and nodded. "Yes, of course. Just a little nervous, I guess."

Her maid of honor touched her hair, the ends curled and resting on her shoulders. "You look pretty. And this is so romantic. You never said a word about him before the last couple of weeks," Susie said.

"He was married before," Cassandra said dryly, hoping to deflect her friend's curiosity. She had bought a cream-colored suit for the ceremony at a darling bridal shop in Union Street. The owner had insisted she needed a small hat with a veil. Studying herself in the mirror,

Cassandra knew she did look pretty. The heightened color in her cheeks was not due to makeup, nor was the sparkle in her eyes. She was going to be married in a few hours!

"So the minute he's free, he sweeps you off your feet." Susie gave a huge sigh and laughed in glee. "It's *so* romantic. I wish someone tall, dark and handsome would sweep me off my feet."

Cassandra started to correct Susie, then changed her mind. Let her friend continue to think it romantic. It would only shatter her dreams if Cassandra told her the truth.

"I help, Daddy," Brittany said as she knotted his shoe-laces.

"Thank you, sweetheart. But I think Daddy can tie his own shoes." He lifted the shoe from her hands and struggled with the knot, wondering if it would be faster to just cut the thing and find a new pair of laces.

He heard a giggle from the bathroom. "Ashley, what are you doing?" he called. He should have taken Helen up on her offer to stop by earlier to get the girls. Or insisted the baby-sitter come today. He had magnanimously given her the day off. He was trying to get dressed with both twins underfoot. And both wanted to help. He blamed Cassandra. She'd insisted they attend the wedding. Otherwise they would have stayed with Jennifer and known nothing about it.

"Noffing."

He might be new to parenting, but he was a fast study. Nothing always meant something. He dropped the shoe in the center of the bed to keep it out of Brittany's hands and stormed into the bathroom. Ashley stood on the closed toilet seat, her face slathered in shaving cream.

Her bright blue eyes peered out of white foam appre-
hensively. There was foam everywhere—on the walls,
the mirror, her nightgown. Thank God he'd waited to
dress them.

"Ashley, I told you yesterday not to bother Daddy's
things, didn't I?" he scolded.

"Wanna shave!"

"Little girls don't need to shave. Even little boys
don't need to shave."

Brittany came to the door and laughed. "Snowman,"
she said gleefully. "Me, too."

"No." Jared steered Brittany out of the bathroom and
started to clean Ashley. He couldn't wait until Cassandra
was here. She could watch at least one of the girls. It
had to be easier one-on-one.

At least he hoped so. He wasn't going through all this
just to find out things hadn't improved.

Careful to keep the cream from his dress pants, he
washed Ashley's face and rinsed her hair. Then he sent
her off to her room while he made an attempt to salvage
the bathroom. Tonight Cassie would be using this room.
Would be sleeping in his bed. He paused as he thought
about that. He'd fantasized about sleeping with her since
that night in New York. When he'd mentioned he expected the marriage to be normal in every way, he'd
halfway anticipated an objection. But she had said nothing.

Tonight she'd be his. He could kiss her until they both
were so hot and bothered they didn't know which way
was up. Then he'd bring her to bed and undress her and
make slow love all night long. He had changed the
sheets first thing after he got up this morning. His closet
had been cleared to make room for her clothes. He
pushed some of the bottles on the sink counter to the
left. She could put her things beside them. It had been

a long time since he'd shared with a woman.

"Daddy! Wanna see Cassie."

"I'll be there in a minute." He hoped his daughters slept soundly tonight. Maybe he'd better take them to the park this afternoon to make sure they got plenty of exercise.

Vaguely excited about the day, Jared gave up analyzing why. That was Cassie's job, he thought, smiling wryly. She loved to analyze things, didn't she? He knew he'd made the right decision for his girls. Anything else was just a bonus.

Jared had sent a limo for Cassandra. She climbed into the back as if she'd been doing it all her life. The driver handed Susie in and then placed Cassandra's bags in the trunk.

"This is class. Are you always going to travel by limo?" Susie asked, examining everything.

"Of course not. Jared has a nice sedan. We drove to Sonora in it last weekend."

"The little time we've had since your bombshell hasn't been enough. I want to know everything about this man. You're my best friend. I can't let you get married unless I approve," Susie teased.

"What do you want to know?" Cassandra asked, stalling for time.

"When did you realize you loved him?" The answer came promptly.

"In a meadow in Sonora. Last weekend, just before he proposed."

"Oh, wow. Tell me more."

There was little to tell, Cassandra realized, but she did her best to make her brief courtship sound romantic and happy. She could be excused if she minimized how much time the twins were with them and exaggerated their time alone. They had not really had a date, she realized. She would be married and never get the chance to date Jared. Ignoring the twinge of disappointment, she embellished every meeting, focusing on how he looked, what he said and how her heart melted just looking at him.

Susie was positively glowing by the time the limo stopped at the small chapel. She hugged Cassandra. "I wish you all the happiness in the world," she said as the driver opened the rear door.

Nervously, Cassandra walked beside her friend into the foyer. It was just eleven. The minister greeted her and they exchanged pleasantries. Helen stepped up, smiling broadly. "You wouldn't be a bride without a bouquet." She gave Cassandra a large bouquet of white and pale pink roses, baby's breath and trailing cream-colored ribbons that exactly matched her suit. A smaller bouquet was given to Susie.

Touched by Helen's thoughtfulness, Cassandra hugged the older woman. "Thank you." Tears stung her eyes. Blinking rapidly, she tried to recapture her composure.

"Ready?" Helen asked. When Cassandra nodded, Helen smiled. "One more thing. Jared asked if I'd hold your glasses."

"My glasses? I need them."

"Humor the man, honey. He isn't asking for a lot."

Nodding, Cassandra slipped them off and handed them to Helen. Everything in the distance blurred.

"When the organist begins to play the wedding march, you start up the aisle," the minister said. "Your groom is already there. She'll begin as soon as I'm in place.''

Cassandra nodded again, too choked up to speak. This was her wedding. It would start in only seconds, and she would bind her life to Jared's for all time.

Susie smiled at her and moved to the door, listening for the musical cue. When it came, she opened the door wide.

Startled at all the people, Cassandra hesitated. She knew there couldn't be more than the two dozen or so people they'd discussed, but it seemed like a huge crowd. Every eye was on her. She froze.

"Come on, that's the wedding march," Susie whispered, nudging her.

At the front of the chapel, she saw Jared. He looked so tall and distant. While she could not see him clearly, she knew exactly what he looked like. His dark suit emphasized his dark hair, his tanned skin. She could feel the strength of his gaze from where she stood. Her gaze moved right. He'd asked his grandfather to be best man. She knew Silas must be happy.

Taking a breath, she stepped forward and almost tripped as she spotted two identical little girls peer around their daddy's legs and grin at her. Their dresses were pink, the exact color of the blossoms in her bouquet. Both looked adorable. If nothing else, to be given a chance to raise these children made everything right.

Her heart melted and tears filled her eyes as she started up the aisle behind Susie.

When she reached Jared, he nodded and turned to face the minister.

"Hi, Cassie," Ashley said.

"Hi, yourself," she whispered, smiling at the little girl.

"Dearly beloved," the minister began.

"Up!" Brittany said, standing in front of Cassandra, holding her arms high.

"Me, too," Ashley said.

"Not now!" Jared said quietly.

"They could see better if they were up," Cassandra whispered. She handed Susie her bouquet and reached to lift Brittany. Settling her dress over her arm, she smiled brightly at Jared and faced the minister.

"And you talk about me spoiling them!" Two seconds later, Jared had Ashley in his arms, his expression impassive as if every groom held a toddler in his arms while exchanging vows with his bride.

The minister smiled broadly and began again.

Cassandra's eyes met Jared's. They faced each other as the age-old words were read. When Jared was asked if he'd take Cassandra as his wife, his voice rang out loud and true as he said, "I will."

The girls were quiet, impressed with the solemnity of the ceremony. When the minister asked Cassandra to repeat her vows, her grip tightened on Brittany. She was not only marrying Jared Hunter, she was agreeing to become the mother of these two little girls. It was fitting that they participate in the ceremony.

It was awkward exchanging rings with an armful of baby girl, but it was done.

"You may kiss your bride."

Light flared in Jared's eyes. Slowly he leaned closer until his lips brushed against Cassandra's.

"Daddy kiss Cassie," Ashley announced.

"Me, too." Brittany gave Cassandra a big smack on her cheek. Ashley couldn't be outdone and demanded her father lean over again so she could kiss Cassie.

"I feel very married now," Cassandra said softly, her heart in her throat. It was done.

Susie patted her friend's arm. "Congratulations!" she said. "I brought a camera. Walk down the aisle and greet whomever you have to, then come back for pictures."

Things happened in a blur. Cassandra met a half a dozen people, and hoped she could remember their names. She was glad for the familiar faces of the men and women she worked with and her neighbors, happy they came to share her special day.

Silas looked like an old friend. He hugged her tightly. "Be good to my boy," he said gruffly.

She nodded and blinked. If she got through the day without her emotions tangling up so much they spilled out, she'd be extremely lucky.

Helen had arranged a small luncheon reception at a private club in North Beach. She handed maps to the guests and shooed them on their way. "The bridal couple needs to have their pictures taken. They'll join us soon." She made sure Cassandra knew where the place was, then hurried away.

Susie enlisted the help of Mark from Cassandra's project team to take pictures so Susie could also be in them. She staged every pose, some with Jared and Cassandra alone, others with the twins, the minister and then with herself and Silas. Only when the role of film was used up was she satisfied. "I have another two rolls for the reception," she said as they hurried out.

Cassandra sipped champagne and smiled. She nibbled the buffet luncheon and smiled. Thanking each guest for coming, she smiled. By midafternoon her cheeks hurt, her feet were beginning to ache and she felt light-headed.

But she didn't want the day to end. She was having a wonderful time.

And when they left, it would be to return to Jared's apartment, to begin their new life together.

Several times during the afternoon she caught sight of her wedding ring—a plain gold band, which shone in the light. It felt strange on her finger—and right. Once she looked from it to Jared and found his gaze on her. Heat pumped through her, and she visualized his big bed. Swallowing, she turned away and tried desperately to remember what the conversation was about.

Every time she thought about making this marriage real, normal, as Jared had said, her heart started to pound and her thoughts would become so tangled she hadn't a clue how to think straight. It was Friday. They would go home after their reception, put the children to bed and begin their life together.

In his bed.

Neither had to be to work before Monday. Which meant they had two entire days to do nothing but—

"You look flushed. Too warm in here?" Helen asked.

"No, I'm fine. It's a wonderful reception. I can't believe you put everything together so fast, on such short notice. Everything is so lovely. Of course I know how efficient you are. Jared couldn't manage without you. But this is really above and beyond—" Cassandra stopped abruptly. She'd been babbling. Sneaking another peek at Jared, she was pleased to see him talking with one of his friends. That gave her the opportunity to study him without his knowing it.

He looked as calm as he did in staff meetings. And why not? As far as he was concerned, this was just another deal. A bargain made and carried out. He probably hadn't given tonight a second thought.

But it was all Cassandra could think about. She remembered how warm his fingers had felt against her skin when he tucked back her hair or clasped his hands with hers as they walked together in Columbia. Tonight he'd touch her all over with those same fingers, those masculine hands. Kiss her until she couldn't remember her name.

Suddenly she wished with all her heart that this was truly a normal marriage. That he loved her as much as she loved him. How would she stand it year after year—to want his devotion and receive only courtesy?

He looked up and caught her eye. Smiling, he gestured for her to join him. When she did so, he encircled her shoulders and drew her close. "You about ready to leave?"

"Now?" Panic gripped her.

"We've eaten, spoken to everyone, even cut the cake. Two or three people keep looking at their watches, and I suspect they don't want to be the first to leave. Grandpa needs to get started to get home before dinnertime. Any reason to stay?"

She shook her head. "I guess not. Where are the girls?"

"Grandpa has Brittany. I think Helen took charge of Ashley a while ago."

"Give the woman a raise. She deserves it."

"For taking one of the terrible twins or for today?"

"Both." Bravely Cassandra tilted her head and looked directly into Jared's eyes. "I think it was a lovely reception. The ceremony was beautifully done."

"Even with two squirming girls in arms?"

"They didn't squirm, they were very well behaved."

"No disappointments?" he asked.

''Why would I? The day's been perfect. Susie was enthralled with the limo.''

''And you?''

She nodded. ''Thank you, Jared. It's been perfect.''

''And not over yet.''

Heat licked every cell in her body. ''No, I guess not,'' she said faintly.

Far too soon, they bade farewell to their guests, gathered their little girls and got into the limousine. Settling in the soft leather seat, Cassandra tried to act normal.

''Cassie tell story,'' Ashley said from the seat opposite where Jared had placed her.

''Mommy now,'' Jared said.

''Mommy gone,'' Brittany said.

''Cassie is your mommy now. You can call her mommy,'' Jared explained.

''Mommy?'' Ashley looked around.

''Jared, I think you're confusing them. They can continue to call me Cassie.''

''Then it will get confusing when we have kids of our own. Ashley, Brittany, Cassie is your new mommy. Your first mommy is gone, but Cassie will be your new mommy. Mommy two.''

''Mommy two?'' Ashley tried to understand.

Cassandra couldn't say a word. Her body hummed from his casual comment about their own children.

''Cassie Mommy two?'' Brittany said.

''Yes, Cassie is Mommy two.''

CHAPTER NINE

THE limousine driver carried Cassandra's bags to the apartment. Jared took Brittany, and Cassandra held Ashley's hand as they rode in silence in the elevator. The girls released their hold and ran to the door when they reached the apartment. Jared tipped the driver, unlocked the door and let the girls dash in.

"Go in your room. I'll be there in a minute so you can change," he instructed them. He carried Cassandra's bags inside, then turned to look at her. "Coming?"

Silently, she nodded then reluctantly stepped inside. So much for her dream of her husband carrying her over the threshold of her new home. Closing the door, she tried to act sensibly. This was not a love relationship. She knew with certainty that Jared had never even thought about it.

He carried her luggage to his bedroom. She took off her wispy hat and set it on the table near the door, then headed to the twins' bedroom. Their dresses were so darling, she didn't want to waste a moment getting them off lest they ruin them.

Did every bride feel a bit let down when the festivities ended and real life returned?

"I'll help the girls change," she called.

She was struggling to snap Ashley's jeans when Jared appeared in the doorway.

"I can finish up, if you want to change." He'd already done so. The casual slacks and pullover shirt looked comfortable. But for a moment, Cassandra missed the dark suit. He'd looked breathtakingly handsome today.

"Okay. What did you want to do now? What should I wear?"

"I thought we'd take these two to the park and let them run. They had enough sugar at the reception to make them higher than a kite."

"I won't be long."

"Take time to unpack if you like. We can go ahead and you can find us when you're done," he suggested. "Remember, I've seen how these girls help in packing. I doubt their unpacking technique is much better."

Cassandra murmured agreement and headed for the bedroom. She wasn't precisely sure what she expected, but it wasn't this. She thought there should be something to extend their special day. Maybe a suggestion for a candlelight dinner. He could have taken her to that place he'd mentioned before, where there was dancing. That would have been nice.

She changed into comfortable jeans and a pink top. Exploring his room, Cassandra discovered he'd made space for her clothes in his closet and left two drawers of the small dresser ajar to show they were empty. Hearing the twins and Jared leave, she began to put away her clothes. She fingered his business suits hanging in the large closet and remembered Jared wearing each of them. His scent filled the space so much she almost felt as if he were there.

Lovingly, she hung the cream suit she'd bought especially for today and wondered when, if ever, she'd wear it again. She hung her other suits, then closed the door. The suitcases she stacked near the front door. She remembered Jared mentioned a storage space in the garage area. The cases could be put there later.

Wandering through the apartment, Cassandra tried to impress upon herself that it was her new home. It seemed alien. None of her things were here yet. The master bedroom and bath were on one side of the living area with the twins' room, the guest room and the second bath on the other side. She peeked into the extra room. Jared's live-in housekeeper had left the place immaculate. Had that situation worked, would he have sought Cassandra for marriage?

Probably not, she mused. Shaking off her vague sense of disappointment, she headed for the park.

It was easy to locate her family from the twins' shrieks of laughter. There was a small playground area with swings, climbing apparatus and tall slides. Jared was pushing the girls in the swings. Not high, but to little girls it probably seemed daring. They laughed and shouted to go higher and higher.

"Need help?" Cassandra asked, joining them.

"Want to swing?" he asked, grinning at her. The slight breeze from the bay had tousled his hair, giving him a rakish air. Gradually Cassandra relaxed. She smiled. This would work.

"No, I'll just watch."

"Go slide," Brittany said.

"Whoops." Jared caught her and stopped the swing. "She doesn't seem to understand about letting go before the swing stops."

"I'll take her to the slide. You can keep pushing Ashley," Cassandra said.

He looked at her, his gaze trailing from the top of her glossy black hair and down the length of her. Leaning over, he brushed his lips against hers. "You look pretty, sweetheart."

Cassandra's legs almost gave way. His compliment had been the last thing she expected.

"Thank you," she murmured, more flustered than she should be. But she had never expected Jared to say anything like that. She watched him while she kept an eye on Brittany. He looked younger laughing with his daughter. She was used to the serious businessman. To see him in a different light felt odd. And intimate. None of the other employees at Hunter Associates had seen this side of him. Not even, she suspected, MaryEllen.

Cassandra was as tired as the twins when they headed for home. During the afternoon they'd run, played tag and red light green light and tried every piece of playground equipment.

"A quick dinner and they'll be ready for bed," she murmured as they reached the apartment. She wasn't sure she wouldn't be, also. It had been a long day. And every moment, she'd thought about being in Jared's bed that night. And that they were married.

"I should have asked what you wanted to do about dinner," Jared said as they walked into the kitchen together. "We can find a café if you don't want to cook tonight."

For a moment, Cassandra felt like an old married woman. The ease with which they spent the afternoon proved they were compatible. But the thrumming of her heart had her tied up in knots. She wondered if, after years of living together, she would one day grow used to being with Jared.

"The girls are too tired to go out, don't you think?" she asked as she peered into the refrigerator. It seemed well stocked. "They'd be cranky while we waited for the food at a restaurant. There must be something we can fix that is fast." Besides, it was her wedding night.

If she couldn't go dancing with her new husband, she surely didn't want to be responsible for the twins when they were so tired. "What do they like to eat?"

"Everything. And lots of it."

Cassandra smiled. "They're probably getting ready to grow again. I remember my foster mother always saying when kids eat like there's no tomorrow, it meant time for new clothes and shoes soon." She stopped talking.

"Do you keep in touch with your foster parents?" Jared asked, leaning casually against the wall near the sink, watching her.

She shook her head and withdrew some ground beef from the refrigerator. "Do you have ingredients for spaghetti?"

"Yes. Why not?"

She looked up, surprised he'd even ask. "We weren't close. They saw me as a glorified baby-sitter. I represented whatever the state was paying that month for my care. I never really thought of them as parents—just people watching me until I was old enough to do it myself." She shrugged, trying to make sure none of the hurt showed. She had so longed for love and acceptance.

Suddenly a thought struck her. Whirling to face him, she said, "You don't think Brittany and Ashley will feel that way about me, do you?"

Slowly Jared unfolded his arms and straightened. He took the three steps necessary to reach her and shook his head. "They love you already. And you love them. It shows, Cassie. You will be the only mother they'll ever know or remember. They'll love you always."

He took the meat from her hands and put it on the counter. Threading his fingers through her shiny hair, he tilted her head until she faced him.

"Thank you for becoming their mother."

His gaze touched every inch of her face.

"The sun kissed your cheeks. They're pink. And your black hair looks like it has light shining through it. There are sparkles in your eyes that remind me of starlight. And your mouth has tempted me all day." He captured that tempting mouth with his, moving over her lips with mastery.

Cassandra reached out and drew his body close to hers until she was nestled against his hard length. She felt as if she were flying. Breathless with delight, she wished the moment could continue forever. Daringly she began to respond, to kiss him back, opening her lips to his quest, letting her tongue dance with his. She hoped he was as excited about kissing her as she was about him holding her. She would die if she couldn't bring him the same pleasure.

Jared released her mouth to trail kisses along her jaw. His fingers tipped her head back and he rained kisses along her throat. His tongue licked, his lips nibbled and his hands kept her still for his pleasure. The minutes ticked by until Cassandra could think of nothing but Jared and the delight she found in his arms. Her blood was boiling, her breathing almost nonexistent. Whirling sensations crested and splashed. Could one person contain such happiness?

She opened her eyes to find his staring into hers. Her love for him was so strong she thought she'd burst.

"We'd better get something for those two or we'll have raving maniacs tormenting us to death in about ten minutes," he said.

She came back to earth with a crash.

Preparing dinner, Cassandra felt as if she existed in some kind of time warp. She was reminded of her first night in New York after being coerced into traveling there with Jared. Hadn't he practically coerced her into this marriage?

That wasn't fair. She'd gone into it with her eyes wide open.

After the girls ate, Cassandra went to run their bath while they helped Jared clean up. Once they were ready for bed, all of them gathered together to read a story. It didn't take the twins long to fall asleep.

Cassandra delayed leaving the girls' room as long as possible. Her heart raced in her chest, and she found it difficult to focus on anything. The minutes passed and each one brought her that much closer to bedtime. And Jared's huge bed.

Wondering if Jared was as anxious as she was, she at last turned and headed for the living room. She wondered no more. He sat in one of the easy chairs, reading reports from work!

This was their wedding night, and he was working!

But of course to him the day had meant nothing beyond a convenient new mother for the sake of his daughters. She cleared her throat.

Looking up, he put the papers on his lap and gestured to the sofa.

"What are we doing with the girls on Monday?" Cassandra asked as she sat down.

"I believe Jennifer is still planning to be here."

"I thought we might look into day care for them, where there are other little children. It would be good for them to interact with others their age. Another advantage would be that we wouldn't be dependent on a single person who could get sick or choose not to come for some other reason."

"Jennifer seems reliable. And if she can't make it one day, you or I could stay home with them. There's been enough disruption in their lives. I'd rather not do day care just yet."

Cassandra nodded and looked out the window. Jared made sense. There had been a lot of disruption in their lives over the last few weeks. And in her own, as well.

"I almost forgot." Jared reached into the briefcase beside his chair and withdrew a large envelope. He tossed it to Cassandra.

"What is this?" she asked, slipping her finger beneath the flap. She withdrew the legal documents and saw shares of Hunter Associates in her name.

"I thought we were going to wait," she said slowly.

"I keep my bargains, Cassie. That was part of the deal. Why wait?" he asked.

Part of the deal. Had she let herself confuse his earlier kiss with genuine caring? Slowly, feeling drained and tired, Cassandra rose. She tucked the stock certificates in the envelope and turned toward the hallway. "I'm tired. I'm going to bed."

But not in his bed. There were limits, and Cassandra had just reached hers. No pretending that this was a love match. No more expecting that life would have a happy ending. She had agreed to this marriage and would live up to her end—acting as a mother to Ashley and Brittany. But she would continue to work hard and make a life for herself apart from watching children.

"I'll be along in a few minutes," Jared said.

She gathered her nightie and used the twins' bathroom to brush her teeth. She slipped into the guest room and didn't bother with a light. She pulled back the covers, thankful to see it freshly made up, and climbed in. Huddling beneath the light blanket, she turned her back to the door and tried to sleep. Images of the day danced behind her eyelids—Susie's excitement, the twins peering around their father's legs, the reception, the afternoon at the park. She'd never spent much time daydreaming about a wedding day, so she couldn't be disappointed. It had been a nice ceremony, with all the proper touches, including Jared's kiss. But the kiss before dinner was the one she remembered.

The overhead light flashed on.

"What the hell are you doing in here?" Jared's angry voice demanded. "I had to look over the entire apartment for you."

She rolled on her back, narrowed her eyes against the sudden light and looked at him. "I said I was going to sleep. I'm tired."

"This is not my bed." He ground out the words.

"No, but it's mine," she returned, sitting up to face him. If they were going to have this out now, she wanted to be in a better position. Maybe she should stand. No, her nightgown was too filmy for that.

"What are you talking about? You know I expected this marriage to be normal in every way. Including sleeping together. We talked about it."

"No, Jared, *you* dictated what *you* wanted. I hardly know you. You don't know me. I understand what you want, and after we get to know each other—"

"What better way to know each other than to sleep together?"

"Not tonight."

He hesitated, his eyes boring into hers. "When, then?" His voice sounded calm, but Cassandra detected the hint of anger.

"When we know each other better," she said bravely. Her heart pounded as she surreptitiously wiped damp palms against the blanket. "We married. I'm the

mommy of your girls. I'll fulfill my part of this marriage
deal.''

''But not tonight?''

She shook her head.

Jared stared at her for another moment, then spun
around, left and slammed the door behind him. As soon
as he heard the sound, he stopped. Listened. Had he
woken the girls? Only silence.

He walked down the hall and hesitated at the door to
his bedroom, but closed it quietly. He wanted to slam it
as hard as he could to dissipate some of the anger that
roiled inside. He'd expected to find Cassie waiting in his
bed a few moments ago. Thinking he was being courteous, he'd let her use the bathroom first. Get ready first.
When he'd come into the room, it was as empty as he'd
left it on the way to their wedding.

Dammit, what was she doing? He'd made it perfectly
clear that he wanted a normal marriage. Had she married
him for the shares of stock? Now that she had that, she
didn't feel compelled to do more. He should have held
off on giving them to her. Yet hadn't she suggested that
very thing? Maybe it wasn't the stock.

Was she shy? he wondered.

Not if her kiss in the kitchen earlier had been anything
to go by. He could still feel her hands on his back, tracing his muscles, clutching him tightly against his sweet
little body. He thought to have her in his bed tonight,
that sexy body bared and pressed against every inch of
him. The longer he thought about it, the angrier he became. Maybe he should go back and get her. Demand
she share his bed. Show her from the first how their
marriage would be.

Slowly the anger drained away. He wouldn't do that.
If she didn't come willingly, he didn't want her at all.

He'd had enough indifference with MaryEllen to last a lifetime. He couldn't do it a second time.

It was only one night. Tomorrow he'd insist she sleep in here with him. Jared headed for the bathroom. He'd take a cold shower and see if he could fall asleep.

In the morning, when Jared entered the kitchen, Cassandra greeted him with a bright smile and a distant, reserved manner he had never seen before. The girls were already dressed and making inroads into cinnamon toast. Their juice had been poured, and from the orange mustaches on matching faces, already sampled. Jared watched Cassandra as she bustled around. He wanted her. Nothing had changed from last night. She was his wife, and she hadn't even given him a good-morning kiss.

"Want eggs or something?" she asked.

"What are you having?" He pulled out a chair and sat, fascinated by her. The jeans fit her bottom snugly, outlining her curves and shapely legs. Her loose T-shirt draped her torso, drifting over the soft shape of her breasts. She'd left her hair down and her glasses off. Color stained her cheeks. He felt a quick kick of desire.

With a glance at the twins, Jared knew there was no way to get Cassandra alone right now. But he wanted her. And he meant to have her today, one way or the other. He'd had more trouble than he expected falling asleep last night. Tonight, things would be different.

"I already ate. I woke up early." She avoided looking at him. "But I can fix you anything."

"I'll have cinnamon toast like the girls," he said. "And coffee."

She nodded and placed a steaming mug before him. "I had the coffee ready," she said.

He caught her wrist before she could draw away and looked up, meeting her eyes. Color rose in her cheeks. Jared almost smiled. She wasn't indifferent, after all. What had last night been about? Slowly he tugged, pulling her down for a kiss.

She tasted sweet and cinnamony. Conscious of the twins avidly watching, he kept the brush of lips light. But it only whetted his appetite for his wife. He wanted more than a light kiss first thing in the morning.

"I thought we might go to the zoo today," Jared said as he watched Cassie prepare his toast.

"Take the girls. I have to go home."

The unexpected reply hit him hard. "What do you mean?"

"I wanted to use this weekend to finish packing everything. I have a moving company coming on Monday to take my furniture to storage. But there are things I want to bring here."

Jared didn't realize how tense he'd been until he felt his muscles relax. She wasn't leaving, just going to get her things. After the weekend, this apartment would be her home. She would have nowhere else to go. A deep sense of satisfaction filled him.

"We can help, if you like."

She smiled at the twins. "I don't think so. I can manage fine by myself. You take the girls."

She was driving him crazy, Jared thought on Thursday morning as he tilted back in his chair in his office and gazed at the San Francisco Bay. From the whitecaps that dotted the expanse, he knew it was windy. But the sun shone and the air was crystal clear. He wished his life was as pristine as the view.

He still slept alone. Every night she'd come up with

some excuse and reiterated the one that they didn't know each other well enough. But how she expected them to get to know each other was a mystery to him. She'd spent the entire weekend packing. Monday night she'd gone to clean the apartment so she could get the security deposit back. Hell, he'd just given her twenty percent of Hunter Associates, and she wanted her security deposit returned.

Tuesday he'd been tied up dealing with the situation in Bangkok. By the time he'd reached home, she'd been asleep. Or feigning sleep, he wasn't sure which. Last night, she'd brought work home and stayed up long after he headed for bed.

Every day she remained friendly, but the wall between them seemed to grow thicker. What happened to his expectations of a docile wife, one so grateful for the Hunter stock she'd be more than willing to fall in with his plans?

He sipped his coffee and shook his head. Cassie wasn't any more likely to fall in with anyone's plans than he was. She had definite ideas of how things should be. Was that part of the problem? Had their marriage not measured up in some way?

But how could that be? It was a business arrangement first, last and always. What was there not to measure up? She received her shares of the stock, he obtained a mother for his kids.

"And what did I get out of it?" he asked aloud. "I want a wife." He'd been accommodating these last few days. But a deal was a deal, and Cassie was welching on her end. Time to stop it. Tonight he'd get the twins to bed early and make sure his wife was in his bed where she should have been all week.

Anticipation began to simmer as he looked forward to the evening.

Cassandra arrived home minutes before Jared. He had suggested they drive together, but after Tuesday, when he'd been so late coming home, she outright refused. She didn't want to be stuck at work if he ran late, and it was likely there'd be occasions when she'd be late and didn't want to hold him up. One of the two of them had to get home each day when the baby-sitter was due to leave.

She spoke with Jennifer for a few minutes, then hugged the twins and invited them to come with her while she changed. They talked excitedly about their day. Jennifer had taken them to the park, and they told Cassandra about seeing a dog. Was it the first one they'd seen? she wondered.

Cassandra had just slipped off her blouse and skirt when Jared appeared in the door. The sound of the children talking had masked any other noise. He held his suit jacket over his shoulder by one finger. Raising an eyebrow, he let his gaze scan her scantily clad figure, a slow, sexy smile holding her enthralled.

Cassandra gathered her casual clothes and fled to the bathroom. Closing the door behind her, she heard the girls greet their father. Blood pounding through her veins, she leaned against the wall and tried to analyze the feelings that coursed through her. His gaze had felt like a touch. She was agonizingly aware of each inch of bare skin glowing with heat. She dressed, then delayed leaving the safety the bathroom afforded. How long could she stall?

The knock on the door answered her silent question. She opened it and gazed at Jared.

He smiled sardonically and leaned over to kiss her gently. "Tonight, Cassandra. I will accept no excuses, no refusals." His voice burned through her.

Involuntarily her eyes shifted to the big bed. The girls were bouncing on it. It still looked huge. She'd never even sat on the side. But tonight, it didn't look as if she'd have a choice.

She opened her mouth, but his was there before she could say a word. He kissed her again, then gently moved her outside the bathroom and closed the door in her face.

Dinner seemed to fly by. Cassandra tried to delay its finish, but that proved impossible with the twins anxious to play for a short while before bath and bed. Even the dishes were finished in record time.

Jared's implacable gaze just about drove her crazy. He watched her through dinner as if she would try to run away. He leaned against the counter while she did the dishes, discussing various projects at the company, asking for her input. He helped with the children's bathing, and the four of them sat on the sofa for reading. But tonight, Cassandra's voice wouldn't work. She insisted Jared read to the children.

The sound of his voice affected her nervous system as strongly as did his touch. She closed her eyes and listened to his rich tones bring the story alive for his daughters. All too soon he finished. It was time to put the children to bed.

Cassandra wanted to crawl into bed with Ashley, pull the baby's blanket over her head and hide away the night. But Jared was right there with her, and when the last kiss had been given, his hand gripped her arm.

"Come with me."

Cassandra's heart pounded. She could see nothing but

Jared, the implacable tilt of his jaw, the tight features of his face. His hand didn't hurt, but his grip was strong enough to make drawing away impossible.

In their bedroom, he closed the door and hauled her into his arms.

Before Cassandra could protest, his mouth found hers and began a sultry assault that left her helplessly excited. Her protests died as she returned his kiss, matching passion for rising passion. Her fingertips traced his jaw, felt the slight rasp of beard. Sensory overload threatened to overwhelm her when her fingers threaded in his thick hair. His mouth did wondrous things to her until she thought she would go insane with wild and exotic longing.

CHAPTER TEN

THE pounding on the door sounded like a shot.

"Daddy, want water!"

"Dammit," Jared said beneath his breath. He opened his eyes and gazed at Cassandra. "Don't move," he ordered.

He opened the door. "Ashley, honey, you should be in bed."

"I'm firstee."

"Okay, just a little water."

"Me, too." Brittany came up the hall, dragging her blanket. "Me, too."

"I guessed as much," Jared said dryly.

Cassandra stepped beside him. "Come on, baby girls, we'll get some nice cold water and then tuck you up in bed again."

"I wanna story," Ashley said when Jared picked her up and carried her into the kitchen. Cassandra brought both girls small glasses of water. She watched them drink without lifting her gaze to Jared. He watched, wondering if she thought by ignoring him she could change anything. Frustration touched him. First the interruption, now Cassandra's coolness. It was enough to drive a man crazy.

"This time stay in your bed," Jared said as he scooped up one twin. He looked at Cassandra. "Coming?"

She shook her head. "You can tuck them in without me."

176

He hesitated, wondering if she planned to bolt from the apartment while he was busy with the girls. Deciding not to press the issue, he shrugged and held out a hand for his other daughter. ''I'll tuck you in, and this time you go straight to sleep, all right?'' he said as they walked down the hall.

Once they were settled, Jared headed for the kitchen. Cassandra was not there. Had she returned to the bedroom? Jared turned and saw her sitting in a chair in the living room. He paused in the archway. She looked like she meant to stay there for quite some time. She met his gaze and never looked away, but by the determined tilt to her chin Jared knew she wasn't ready to take up where they had left off.

''I want to talk to you,'' she said and pointed to another chair. ''Please.''

He crossed the room and sat where she indicated. What he wanted to do was pull her from the chair, sling her across his shoulders and take her to their room. This time he'd make sure the door was locked and not let anything interfere. But she seemed firmly ensconced in the chair.

''About what?'' he asked, hiding his frustration with difficulty.

''About work, us, our marriage. Different things.'' She swallowed hard. Try as she might to hide it, Jared could spot her nervousness from his seat. Slowly he leaned back, curious what she might have to say. For a moment his business sense took over. How would she be at negotiations? MaryEllen had been a natural, but Cassandra seemed too soft, too nice.

''So talk.''

She cleared her throat. ''I was going to wait for

Saturday. I thought it might be better, but now I guess I have to tell you tonight.''

Uncertainty hit Jared. He focused on Cassie, forgetting instantly about work, negotiating skills and his first wife.

"Tell me what?"

She cleared her throat again. "I'm returning the shares of Hunter Associates. I have thought about it all week, and truly I don't want them.''

"Why not? I thought that was what you did want, part ownership in a business. You said so.''

Nodding, she agreed. "But not handed to me. I don't feel I've earned the shares. And that's what I really want—to feel I've earned my way. To be paid because I agreed to become your wife is cheating us both. I don't want them, Jared.''

He listened, stunned. Did she mean to end the marriage as well as the partnership? Suddenly he knew he couldn't allow that. He had to make her see they couldn't end their marriage. The girls would be devastated.

"So what do you want?"

"Actually, I want to look for a new job," she said.

"What?" He stood up and glared at her. "What are you talking about? You can't leave the company!" The news shocked him. He strode to the window and gazed out, not seeing anything. How could she even suggest leaving? Was that the first step?

"I can't stay. I'll never know if I'm getting anywhere because my ideas are solid and my experience is growing or because I'm the boss's wife.''

Slowly Jared turned to look at her. She wanted to leave because she was the boss's wife? He knew how important doing well in business meant to her. But he couldn't shake the fear that this was but the first step.

"You are not ending our marriage!" he said.

Her eyes widened in surprise. Shaking her head, she said, "No. I thought we agreed I should be the girls' mother."

"And my wife."

"Well, yes, that, too." She cleared her throat a third time. "Actually I wanted to talk to you about that, as well. Oh, not that I want to end the marriage. We only got married a week ago."

"Some might say the marriage is still pending consummation," Jared remarked dryly.

"I know, and that's the other thing I wanted to talk about."

"Tonight," he said firmly.

"Will you let me talk? This entire business has been rushed. I was convenient and had the child-care experience you needed—"

"Cassandra, just say whatever it is you want to say and let's go to bed."

"That's it, Jared. I'm not ready to go to bed with you. I know men can just hop into bed with whomever, but I can't."

"With whomever?" He took a step closer to her. "Dammit, what do you think I am, some kind of stud who pounces on women whenever I get in the mood? I was married for six years to a business partner. We rarely shared a bed, and that was fine with both of us. But we kept our vows and didn't seek entertainment elsewhere. Then she left, and for the last three of those years I've been alone."

"That's just it. You've been alone and now you're not and you want me."

"You got that part right. I sure do want you."

"You know as well as I do that there is no reciprocal love in this relationship. I think we need more time to get to know each other and develop some kind of friendship before we start sleeping together," she said in a rush.

Her words made sense, but the timing was off. She should have said something last week. He couldn't wait for them to become friends. He wanted her more and more each day. The wall she'd built between them since last Friday had grown, not diminished. If he left her to her own devices, would he ever breach it?

He stepped near and held out his hand. "Come with me for a minute. Just a minute."

She hesitated, then took his hand. She stood so close he could smell the faint scent of roses she always wore. It teased his senses and made him more aware of her than ever. She was petite, just reaching his shoulder. Her figure was dainty and feminine and drew him like a magnet drew iron. But he had an idea she hadn't a clue how he felt.

He walked with her into the bedroom, ignoring the bed and moving to stand before the full-length mirror near the closet. He pulled her in front of him and looked at her in the mirror.

"Look at yourself and tell me you don't understand why I want you. Only you. Your hair is beautiful, shiny and thick and soft as a baby's." Slowly his fingers threaded in the wavy strands, reveling in the silky feel. He didn't know how she kept it so pretty, but it was. He pulled it from her face, letting the tresses slip over and through his fingers, relishing the sensations. His eyes met hers.

"Your skin resembles peaches and cream. You're so

young you don't have a single wrinkle yet, and the texture is as pure as the finest porcelain." His index finger lightly grazed her cheek. Instantly her color deepened, and Jared felt the pull of attraction grow stronger. "I love it when you blush. Most women these days are incapable, but the slightest thing sets you off."

She closed her eyes with a groan.

He leaned forward to whisper in her ear, "Shyness in this liberal society is uncommon and all the more precious for being so."

Opening her eyes a slit, she looked at the reflection of the two of them.

Jared kept his face beside hers, his mouth just inches from her ear. Resting his hands on her shoulders, he let his gaze blatantly follow the shapely contours of her body. "You are feminine and sexy, Cassie. I've wanted you since that first night in New York. The first time you slipped off your glasses, I was gone. Your eyes are dark and mysterious and drive me wild. Sometimes you look at me as if you know something I don't know. Other times you look at me as if I'm someone special, still other times like I'm the biggest idiot on the face of the earth. I love the special times best."

Tears flooded those eyes, and Jared hesitated. But when she smiled, he continued.

"When I look at you, I see the future, our future. We may never have that reciprocal love you spoke of, Cassie, but we can have a strong bond. I want to spend my life with you, and making love with you will be a part of it. But not because you are just some woman who happens to be passing by. It's only because you are who you are. Sexy, enticing, enthralling."

"Jared, no one has ever said one of those things about me. Are you trying some masterful selling technique here?'' she murmured, leaning against him, her hands coming to cover his on her shoulders.

Slowly he slid his palms across the front of her, passing her breasts till they rested on her waist. He didn't miss her shiver.

"I'm good at selling things. I hope I'm selling you on why I want you in my life. If you want to become friends first, I guess I can wait. But it's going to be hard. And I want you to know how hard, just like I'll know it every day until you say yes."

Cassandra felt awed he'd given her so much power. Studying their figures in the mirror, she knew she'd love him until she died. No one had ever said such wonderful things about her. Her body felt feverish. She longed for Jared, for his kisses, for the touch of his hands. Should she keep denying what they both wanted? How important was love, anyway? Didn't she have enough for both of them? She'd married him knowing there was none on his part. Nothing had changed. She could explore the reaches of passion with this man. He'd take care of her. Just as he planned to take care of his daughters.

"I love you, Jared," she said softly.

He jerked and his eyes widened. Slowly he smiled. "If that's what I get for pointing out your good features, I should have mentioned them earlier."

"I've loved you since before tonight," she said softly, her gaze holding his in the mirror.

He turned her in his arms and gazed directly at her. "Cassie, I—"

She covered his mouth with her fingertips. "No, don't say anything. We married for our own reasons. I have changed my mind about ownership in Hunter Associates, but not anything else. I thought I needed some more time to be your wife, but I don't. Not after this." Moving her hand to the back of his head, she pulled him down for a kiss, as hot and wild as she could make it.

The room spun when he lifted her and settled into a rainbow of delight when he laid her on the big bed. Tonight, he'd said. Tonight it was.

A thundering herd of elephants charged up the hall. Cassandra came awake and sat up before the stampede could trample her.

"Daddy, Daddy, Daddy," the twins chanted as they pounded on the door.

Falling back in relief, she turned her head slightly and met the twinkling eyes of her husband. Cassandra knew heat flooded her cheeks—she could feel it—but she refused to look away. After his words of last night, she didn't care if he saw her shyness or embarrassment. After his loving touch and caresses, she didn't care much about anything except experiencing them again.

"Cassie, Cassie, Cassie." The pounding became even louder.

"I think our daughters are awake," Jared said slowly, his hand coming to cup Cassie's cheek, his thumb tracing delicate paths on her skin.

"Are you sure there are only two little girls out there? It sounded more like a stampeding herd."

He laughed. "Get something on, and I'll let in the herd." He rose and drew on a pair of pajama bottoms. Waiting only long enough for Cassandra to drop a nightgown over her head, he opened the door. The twins danced in, peeking around him to see Cassandra in the big bed. They made a beeline for her and clamored to get up.

Jared watched, unable to believe his life had changed so drastically the last few weeks. Before leaving for

Bangkok, he'd been for all intents and purposes a bachelor. Now he had a wife and two daughters. The feeling hit him hard. The realization a revelation.

He loved them.

All of them.

His gaze sought Cassandra's. No wonder he'd almost panicked last night when she said she didn't want shares. He feared she wanted to end their marriage. And he knew that he could never let her go. Not because she'd make the girls a wonderful mother. He couldn't let her go because his life would be nothing without Cassandra Hunter in it!

"What?" she asked, smiling at something Brittany had said. Slowly her smile began to fade. "Is something wrong?"

"I don't think so," Jared said. For the first time in years, everything seemed perfect. He had a wife who loved him and his daughters. And he loved her. He envisioned their future. They would build a strong bond, forged in a reciprocal love, not merely mutual interests as he'd once so arrogantly thought.

"I love you, Cassie," he said softly.

Her eyes flooded with tears as she gazed at him. "Truly?"

"Cassie sad?" Brittany said, snuggling closer.

"Mommy two," Ashley said loudly, then patted Cassandra's arm. "Mommy two sad?"

"No, actually, I'm so happy I think I'll burst," Cassandra said as the tears ran down her cheeks. Her gaze never wavered from Jared's.

He crossed the room and gathered her into a tight embrace, kissing her hard.

"Me, too, Daddy, kiss me, too," Brittany said, pushing against him.

"Tonight, we'll see if Jennifer can stay and we'll go to dinner. We need some time alone."

She nodded, clutching his shoulder as if she'd never let go.

"Marco's, where there's dancing," Jared said.

"Sounds great."

"Then we'll come home and these two will be asleep and we can—"

Her fingers covered his mouth. "I know exactly what we can do. Do you really love me?"

"With all my heart. I realized it when I saw you with the twins. I love them so much, and then I realized I loved you as much—differently, but every bit as strong."

"That's why I married you, you know," she said softly. "I knew when you asked me in the meadow that I loved you. I was slow in responding, and you rushed in with the offer of shares. Haven't you told us at work never to rush negotiations?"

He smiled, shifted slightly to accommodate the two little girls who wanted to be included in his arms. "I couldn't take the chance you'd say no. And I don't want you to say no to my next suggestion."

"The way I feel right now, I doubt I could deny you anything," she said, smiling radiantly.

"Keep the shares. Learn as you go with the company. I can't have my wife working for a competitor. Remember, MaryEllen and I were about your age when we started out. We didn't know that much but learned as we went along. Stay, Cassie. Stay and build Hunter Associates with me and the girls."

"Do you think I should?" she asked.

"Absolutely." He leaned forward to kiss her again.

"I can't believe it. I wish we had told each other this

a week ago. Do you realize this is the first-week anniversary of our wedding?"

"As soon as we can get things straight at work, we'll take off for a real honeymoon. Just the two of us."

"I thought you married me to watch these two." She indicated the squirming girls.

"That's the reason I told you. Sooner or later Helen would have found someone who could live in. I may even have thought that was the reason for a few days. But this last week has proved I want more than a babysitter. I want you, for yourself, because I love you! Forever."

She hugged him tightly. "I love you, Jared. I will forever."

"Hug me, Mommy," Ashley demanded, not to be slighted.

"Me, too," said Brittany.

Don't miss your chance to read
award-winning author

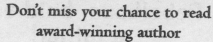

PATRICIA POTTER

First Scottish historical romance

THE ABDUCTION

An eye for an eye. Clan leader Elsbeth Ker longed
for peace, but her stubborn English
neighbors would have none
of it—especially since the
mysterious Alexander had
returned to lead the
Carey clan. Now the
crofters had been
burned out, and the
outraged Kers demanded
revenge. But when Elsbeth faced her enemy,
what she saw in his steel gray eyes gave her pause....

Look for *THE ABDUCTION* this March 1999,
available at your favorite retail outlet!

HARLEQUIN®
Makes any time special ™

Coming Next Month

#3551 MAIL-ORDER MARRIAGE Margaret Way
All that was missing from Matthew Carlyle's life was the right woman to share his Outback cattle-station home. Short on time to socialize, he'd advertized for a wife. City-born Cassandra Sterling had answered him, but how serious about marriage could this poor little rich girl be?

#3552 THE BOSS AND THE BABY Leigh Michaels
Four years ago, Lucas Hudson had dismissed Molly's feelings for him as infatuation—how could she now work for him? She would have to swallow her pride and think of the three-year-old daughter she had to support. But how long would it take Lucas to realize that he'd left Molly with more than a broken heart—that he'd left her with their baby?

Marrying the Boss: *From boardroom...to bride and groom!*

#3553 UNDERCOVER BABY Rebecca Winters
Diana Rawlins has turned up at the hospital with amnesia and a baby in her arms! She doesn't remember how either of them happened. Her husband, Cal, is determined to get to the bottom of the mystery—especially as that seems to be the only way he can save his marriage!

Love Undercover: *Their mission was marriage!*

#3554 LOVE & MARRIAGE Betty Neels & Emma Goldrick
Help celebrate Harlequin's fiftieth anniversary in style with this special two-in-one volume from two of our most popular Romance authors.

"MAKING SURE OF SARAH" by Betty Neels
Having fallen in love with Sarah at first sight, Dr. Litrik ter Breukel vowed to go slowly because of her youth and innocence. But perhaps he'd taken things too slowly—it seemed to him that she'd found another man! Now it was up to Sarah to put him right, and it was up to Litrik to propose!

"SOMETHING BLUE" by Emma Goldrick
What could a girl say when her ex-husband turned up out of the blue and asked her to marry him—again? That was the problem facing Marne when Rob suddenly re-proposed. But did he still want only a convenient wife?